W9-BXR-783

FICTION
Hap

Hapka, Cathy.

Chasing gold

DUE DATE	MCN	11/14	17.99

TWEEN FICTION HA

Chasing Gold

MARGUERITE HENRY'S

Ponies *of* Chincoteague

♦ Chasing Gold ♦

CATHERINE HAPKA

Aladdin

New York   London   Toronto   Sydney   New Delhi

ALADDIN

An imprint of Simon & Schuster Children's Publishing Division
1230 Avenue of the Americas, New York, NY 10020
This Aladdin hardcover edition November 2014
Text copyright © 2014 by The Estate of Marguerite Henry
Jacket illustration copyright © 2014 by Robert Papp
Also available in an Aladdin paperback edition.

For information about special discounts for bulk purchases, please contact
Simon & Schuster Special Sales at 1-866-506-1949 or business@simonandschuster.com.
The Simon & Schuster Speakers Bureau can bring authors to your live event.
For more information or to book an event contact the Simon & Schuster Speakers Bureau
at 1-866-248-3049 or visit our website at www.simonspeakers.com.
Book design by Karina Granda
The text of this book was set in Adobe Caslon Pro.
Manufactured in the United States of America 1014 FFG
2 4 6 8 10 9 7 5 3 1
Library of Congress Control Number 2014944360
ISBN 978-1-4814-0344-3 (hc)
ISBN 978-1-4814-0342-9 (pbk)
ISBN 978-1-4814-0343-6 (eBook)

Chasing Gold

◆ CHAPTER ◆

1

"EASY, WINGS," HALEY DUNCAN MURMURED, shortening the reins to stop her pony from leaping into a canter as they crossed through an open gate into a large pasture. "We're supposed to be doing trot sets this morning, remember? That means we need to actually, you know, *trot*."

The pony's left ear swiveled back toward her, then focused once again on the large sycamore log lying halfway up a gentle slope just ahead. The log's dappled bark was further dappled by shade from the rising sun hitting the tree line outside the pasture fence, making it look odd, but Haley knew that Wings wasn't staring at the log because he was afraid. He wanted to jump it!

Haley smiled as Wings trotted sideways in protest against her snug rein. This field was one of their favorite places to practice cross-country jumping. Haley, with help from her uncle and cousins, had built several sturdy practice jumps there over the past couple of years, and she couldn't count the number of times she and Wings had schooled over their handmade cross-country course— sometimes with only wild birds and rabbits for company, like now, and other times dodging the feeder calves that rotated through this and several other pastures on her family's Wisconsin farm.

Wings snorted and tossed his head. His trot got springier as he tried again to move forward into a canter. It was obvious that he thought jumping was a much better idea than boring trot sets.

"Oh, all right, you convinced me," Haley said with a laugh. One of the things she loved about the lively Chincoteague pony was that he never kept his opinions to himself. "I suppose it couldn't hurt to do just one. . . ."

She loosened the reins and the pony immediately surged into a canter, his gaze fixed on the log. Haley grinned as they sailed over with at least a foot to spare. Wings loved jumping as much as she did, which made them a great team in their chosen sport of eventing. The feeling of galloping across a field and sailing over a jump, the thrill of flying through the air, totally at one with her horse, was what had gotten Haley hooked on the sport in the first place.

But by now, Haley had been eventing long enough to know that loving to jump wasn't enough. They'd never make it above beginner novice level if they spent all their riding time goofing off and jumping logs just for the heck of it, let alone make it to the top of the sport, as Haley dreamed of doing one day.

Wings was already looking at the next jump, a stack of straw bales. But Haley brought him back to a trot and turned him in the opposite direction.

"Sorry, boy." She gave him a pat. "We have work to do. We both need to be fit enough not to embarrass ourselves in front of Zina Charles in a few weeks. Besides, we don't have much time this morning—I still have chores to do before school."

She grimaced, suddenly remembering that she'd promised to take care of both Jake's and Danny's morning chores today in addition to her own. Not that she minded—every time she did her cousins' chores, it was money in her pocket. And she still needed to save up more if she wanted to make it to that clinic.

She still could hardly believe that Zina Charles was holding a clinic so close. Living out in the middle of nowhere, as her friend Tracey called it, Haley knew she was lucky that she only had to haul half an hour to the closest local eventing trainer. And now one of the superstars of the sport was coming to a farm just forty minutes away!

From the first moment she'd heard about it, Haley had been determined to ride in that clinic—no matter what it took. She wasn't afraid of hard work, and she'd barely noticed the extra chores until school had started a couple of weeks earlier. But these days she had to set her alarm early to get everything done, and this particular Tuesday morning she was especially tired, since her babysitting job the night before hadn't ended until almost ten p.m.

Haley yawned and took both reins in one hand so

she could push back the sleeve of her windbreaker. That was another thing that had changed over the past week or two—now that it was September, the weather was already turning, with a definite nip in the air at dawn. As Haley glanced down at her watch, there was a sudden flutter of feathers in an overgrown patch of weeds just ahead. A bird flew out with a squawk, and Wings leaped sideways.

"Hey!" Haley exclaimed as she clenched her legs around the pony to keep her seat. She'd lost both her stirrups, but she stayed centered in the saddle. "You goofball," she added with a laugh as the pony used the spook as an excuse to break into a canter again, tossing in a small buck for good measure. Haley rode through it easily—it was far from the first buck she'd sat through on Wings—and shoved her feet back into the stirrups.

A moment later they were trotting calmly again. But only for a moment. That quick glance at her watch had told Haley that they were running late. With one last wistful look at the inviting field full of jumps, Haley turned Wings around and kicked him into a brisk canter, heading for home.

"Good boy." Haley gave Wings a pat as she slipped off his halter. "I'll see you after school."

The pony nudged at her, clearly hoping for one more chunk of carrot. When none was forthcoming, he turned and ambled off toward the trio of sturdy quarter horses grazing at the far end of the pasture. Haley was glad to see them out there—that meant someone else had turned them out, which meant one fewer chore on her list. Probably Uncle Mike, she figured. No way would the boys bother when they were paying her.

Haley hurried back along the dirt path to the tidy farmyard. At one end stood the barn, its big double doors thrown open to the morning sun. Directly opposite was the rustic white-painted picket gate leading into the back garden of the family's rambling farmhouse. In between, a dozen laying hens and a handsome wyandotte rooster were pecking for bugs and bits of grain in the hard-packed dirt barnyard—Haley had opened the henhouse door on her way to get Wings earlier. Several cats were lounging around the yard, and a portly beagle mix was snuffling at the dirt, probably trying to gobble up whatever bugs were there before the chickens got to them.

As Haley headed for the barn, a different dog trotted out to greet her. Haley loved all animals, but Bandit was her favorite of the gang of cats and dogs on the farm, and he seemed to know it. He was a lean, restless collie mix that had wandered onto a neighbor's property a few years earlier and made a nuisance of himself chasing their sheep. Knowing that Haley and her uncle both had a soft heart when it came to dogs, the neighbor had offered him to them instead of dropping him off at the county pound—or something worse.

"Hey, buddy." Haley scratched around the dog's ruff. Bandit wiggled from head to toe, his long, furry tail thumping against Haley's legs. Then he pulled away, dashing over and grabbing a stick. He brought it to Haley, tail wagging so fast it was almost a blur.

Haley knew she should keep moving if she didn't want Jake to leave for school without her. But she couldn't resist tossing the stick a few times. Bandit chased it with gleeful abandon, barely seeming to notice the chickens squawking as they scattered before him, or the black-and-white cat giving him a dirty look when he almost stepped on her.

"Okay, that's enough," Haley told the dog after a few throws. "Sorry, buddy."

Stifling a yawn, she stood and watched for a moment as two of the hens squabbled over a tasty caterpillar. Bandit sat down on her left foot, as usual wanting to be as close to her as possible. Haley smiled at the familiar feel of his bony rump atop her boot. She couldn't imagine life without Bandit any more than she could imagine not having Wings.

And in a way, the two animals had a lot in common even aside from their energetic natures and devotion to her. The spunky pinto Chincoteague pony had also come from a neighbor, though a different one. He'd been the Smiths' daughter's barrel-racing pony, shipped in from the East Coast as a five-year-old after running away with a series of young kids. When Leah Smith had gone off to college after four or five successful years running barrels, her parents hadn't wanted to sell her pony. Besides, how many people in rural Wisconsin would want a Chincoteague pony with only one speed—fast—and a habit of bucking when he didn't get his way? But Haley had adored Wings from the first time she'd ridden him, and the neighbors had agreed to an indefinite free lease, which meant that Wings could live with Haley for as long as she wanted and come back to the Smiths if she didn't want him anymore. Not that Haley could imagine that ever happening— Wings was definitely a keeper!

Haley's cousins and some of her friends at school still liked to make fun of her choice of sports and breeds, since most of the horse people in these parts rode Western on stocky quarter horses, paints, or Appaloosas. But Haley was in heaven. She'd read and reread *Misty of Chincoteague* so many times she could hardly believe that the cute little pinto in her pasture with the wing-shaped markings across his back was a real, live Chincoteague pony who'd made the swim across the channel from Assateague Island as a foal. It was just a bonus that he jumped as if he'd been born and bred for it!

As Haley was thinking about that, the sudden blast of a car horn nearby made her jump. Despite the early hour, traffic was already zooming by on the busy country highway just a few dozen yards beyond the farm's sturdy woven-wire perimeter fence. Haley yawned again and rubbed her face, then gave Bandit one last pat and got back to work. Riding had woken her up for a while, but yet another early morning was catching up with her. Still, it would all be worth it in a few weeks when she and Wings got to that clinic.

A few minutes later Haley was struggling to balance a wheelbarrow full of manure and open the gate when her seventeen-year-old cousin Jake wandered into the barnyard, hands shoved into the pockets of his baggy jeans.

"Get the gate for me, will you?" Haley called. The muck pile was outside the perimeter fence to make it easier for her uncle to get to with the tractor. That meant opening and closing the sturdy mesh gate for every trip out there so that none of the animals escaped onto the busy road.

Jake grinned, lounging against the hitching rail in the middle of the yard. "Why should I? I'm paying you to do *all* my chores this morning, remember?"

"Just do it!" Haley said, knowing he would.

Jake was like a brother to her, for better and for worse. So was his younger brother, Danny. And Aunt Veronica and Uncle Mike were like parents to Haley—the only ones she remembered, mostly, since her own parents had died in a car crash when Haley was just four years old. Her only memories of them were hazy and dim—her father swinging her up into a battered Western saddle atop an ancient quarter horse for her very first ride; her mother laughing and dancing in the kitchen; the three of them having a picnic in a park in Chicago. Sometimes those memories made Haley feel a little bit sad, as if she should remember more of the four years she'd had with her parents. But her aunt and uncle treated her like one of their own, and that was mostly good enough for her.

Jake opened the gate, shoving Bandit back with his foot to keep the dog from following Haley outside. She dumped the wheelbarrow with one expert move, then hurried back to the gate. Jake swung it open again and then latched it behind her. "Thanks," she said breathlessly.

"Sure." Jake watched her shove the wheelbarrow back into the shed. "Already finish the stalls?"

"Only half." Haley checked her watch. "I'll have to do the rest after school—I still need to check water and feed the chickens. Oh, and I haven't gathered eggs yet. . . ."

"You're making me tired just watching you." To prove it, Jake let out a wide yawn and leaned against a fence post. "I hope this silly English riding thing you're going to is worth it."

"It will be." Haley didn't bother rising to the bait about "silly English riding." She'd heard it all before, and she didn't really care what anyone thought of her sport. "Zina Charles is the best of the best. She was short-listed for the US Olympic Team last time, and she'll probably make it next time. Plus, I hear she's an amazing trainer. Someone posted on one of the online eventing forums that he'd learned more from a one-day clinic with Zina than he did in a year's worth of lessons with anyone else!"

"Hmm." Jake didn't look impressed. "Anyway, Mom sent me out to check on you. I'm leaving in twenty minutes, so don't be late."

Without waiting for a response, he loped off toward

the house. Haley checked her watch again. She knew Jake probably wouldn't actually leave without her, at least not if her aunt was paying attention. But Aunt Veronica wouldn't be happy if Haley made them all late for school. . . .

Minutes later Haley had fed and watered the chickens, topped off the big stock tank in the horses' pasture, and grabbed that morning's eggs from the henhouse. Bandit shadowed her the whole time, his fringed tail wagging.

"Here you go, buddy," Haley said, quickly dumping some kibble into a couple of shallow pans in the barn aisle.

Bandit dove for the food, while the beagle mix and a couple of other dogs raced over to join in. The cats watched with interest, though none of them moved until Haley poured their food into several dishes on top of the big wooden cabinet in the barn office, where the dogs couldn't reach it.

Hurrying out of the office, Haley paused, tempted to grab the broom leaning near the door. But she didn't have time to sweep right now—that would have to wait until after school too, unless Aunt Veronica did it for her before then. Feeling slightly guilty for leaving chores undone, she raced into the house. She grabbed a waffle off the platter on the table, wolfing it down dry as she sprinted up the creaky steps to her small bedroom overlooking the back garden.

As she was pulling on her school clothes, Haley wandered over to look at the flyer pinned to the bulletin board over her desk. It was the information sheet she'd received in the mail after sending in her deposit for the clinic. There was a picture of Zina Charles at the top, and below that were the time, location, and contact info for the clinic.

Haley finished yanking her shirt on over her head, then reached out and touched the flyer with her fingertips. "I'll see you soon, Zina," she whispered with a smile.

Glancing down, she noticed her laptop lying on her desk where she'd dumped it the afternoon before. She hadn't touched it since then, thanks to that babysitting job. Which meant she hadn't logged on to the Pony Post in almost twenty-four hours.

The Pony Post was a private message board Haley had started along with three other girls. She considered the other members among her very best friends, even though the four of them had never met in person. Maddie

Martinez lived in California, Nina Peralt in New Orleans, and Brooke Rhodes in Maryland, just a short distance across the Virginia state line from Chincoteague. The four of them might never have met except for one thing—they all loved and rode Chincoteague ponies. The Pony Post was a place where they could share that interest, along with photos and stories about their ponies and the rest of their lives.

When Haley logged on to the Pony Post, she found several new posts from the others. She skimmed them as she pulled on her socks. Most were just the usual chit-chat about the other girls' ponies and such, but a few were aimed at Haley.

> [MADDIE] Hey Haley, thought of u today—
> Ms. Emerson offered to take some of us from
> the barn to watch a big local three-day event
> as a field trip! I told everyone I know someone
> who events, and they were all totes impressed!
>
> [NINA] Sounds fab, Mads! Just think—

someday it'll be Haley riding in those big events. We can say we knew her when!

[BROOKE] Have u saved up enough for the ZC clinic yet, Haley? I know u were worried about that. It's coming up pretty soon, right?

[NINA] But we know you can do it! You'll make it to that clinic and blow ZC away! She'll probably want to hire u as her groom and apprentice.

[MADDIE] & she'll prolly be so impressed w/Wings that she'll try to buy him so she can ride him in the next Olympics!

[BROOKE] But Haley will never sell— she & Wings are a team!!!

[MADDIE] Of course she won't sell. I'm just saying. Anyway, Haley, check in when u can and let us know what's up and how we can help!

Haley smiled. Maybe nobody around here understood how excited she was to ride with Zina Charles. But at least her Pony Post friends were just as thrilled about it as she was!

She clicked open a text box, thinking about how to respond. Just then she heard her aunt hollering her name.

Oops. Haley realized it was time to go. Writing back to her Pony Post friends would have to wait a little longer.

"Coming!" Haley shouted, tucking the laptop under her arm and heading for the stairs.

◆ CHAPTER ◆

2

HALEY YAWNED AS SHE SPUN THE COMBI-
nation lock on her locker. She was so tired that she had
to do it three times before it clicked. As she swung the
locker open, she glanced at the collage of pictures she'd
taped inside the door. There were several photos of
Wings. Her favorite one showed him wading in the farm
pond, which reminded her of his Chincoteague heritage.
There were also a couple of pictures of her and Wings
jumping various things, including her aunt's favorite garden bench. Danny had taken that one—he was actually a
pretty good amateur photographer.

More recently, Haley had added a big picture of Zina

Charles that she'd clipped out of a magazine. It showed Zina aboard one of her horses, a big bay with a wide blaze and a bold expression. The two of them were jumping an impressive-looking trakehner at last spring's Rolex Kentucky Three-Day, the most prestigious event in the United States.

"I'm getting there, Zina," Haley murmured, brushing her fingers across the picture. She couldn't wait to meet Zina and soak up everything she could from her. All she needed was a little more money to pay the clinic fee. Then she and Wings would be on their way to moving up the levels. And maybe someday it would be them jumping a huge obstacle in some important competition. . . .

"Yo, Duncan," a voice interrupted Haley's daydreams.

Blinking, she turned and saw Owen Lemke standing there, grinning at her. "Oh," she said. "Hi."

She'd known Owen for as long as she could remember. Not only were they in the same class at school, but he was a rider too. Haley often competed against him when she took Wings to local play days and team pennings. It wasn't eventing, but it was still fun—especially when she and Wings beat out Owen and his fancy registered quarter horse.

"What're you doing?" Owen leaned past her, peering at the pictures in her locker. "Trying to figure out where to get a real horse instead of that weird East Coast thing you've been riding?"

Haley rolled her eyes. "Hardly. And even if I was, you're the last person I'd ask for help."

Owen grinned. "Don't be a hater, just 'cause Chance and I beat you at that penning last month."

"Only because our last cow was a dud. And don't forget, Wings and I beat you the three times before that," Haley countered. "It's nice to have a horse who's good at everything, instead of one who can't do anything except chase cows."

Owen snorted. "What else is there?" he said. "I'd never ask Chance to prance around in a fancy-prancy English saddle. If I did, he'd probably buck me off."

"Probably," Haley agreed with a smirk. "Come to think of it, you're probably better off sticking to Western. If you didn't have the horn to hold on to, you'd probably fall off the first time your horse broke out of a slow Western Pleasure lope."

Owen's friend John appeared just in time to hear the last exchange. "Ooh, burn!" he cried, shoving Owen into the lockers.

"Get out of my face." Owen shoved John back. "What, are you thinking of trading in your cowboy boots for some tight britches, just like Haley?"

"No way!" John shoved Owen again.

Haley rolled her eyes as the two boys continued to trade taunts while they moved off down the hall. She was glad they'd forgotten about her. The teasing about being an English rider was familiar, and normally she didn't mind it. But today she was too tired to come up with good comebacks.

"I told you, Haley!" Tracey exclaimed, rushing over with her blue eyes wide and excited. "Didn't I totally tell you?"

"Tell me what?" Haley dug into her locker, wondering if she'd remembered to stick her math book in her bag before she left home.

Tracey poked her in the arm. "That Owen so obviously likes you!" she said in a loud stage whisper.

"What? Oh, please." Haley sighed. Tracey *had* told her that—probably a million times in the past two weeks, or at least that was how it felt to Haley. What had happened to Tracey this year? When had she turned so boy crazy?

Never mind—Haley knew when it had happened. Over the summer, at the same time Tracey suddenly became interested in clothes and makeup and the latest hairstyles. Before that, she'd been a tomboy just like Haley. In fact, the two of them had always looked enough alike that people often took them for sisters. Tracey's light-brown hair was just a smidge darker than Haley's strawberry blond and tended to get snarled by the wind just as easily. With their matching pointy chins and constantly sunburned noses, they'd been "two peas in a pod," as Uncle Mike always said.

But over the past year, some of that had changed. Tracey still had the pointy chin, but she'd cut her hair shorter and added blond highlights. She'd grown taller, too, spurting up nearly two inches and even adding the beginning of some curves to her skinny frame.

The physical changes in Haley's best friend were weird enough. But it was the other changes that bugged her a lot more. Haley still wasn't sure when she'd first noticed that Tracey was more interested in hiking through the local mall than through the woods, but it had been impossible to ignore after Tracey's older sister had whisked her off down to "the city"—that was what Tracey had started calling Chicago—for a back-to-school haircut at some fancy salon last month.

"I bet he's going to ask you to the dance." Tracey pulled a compact mirror out of her purse and peered into it, poking at her elaborately blow-dried bangs. "Too bad that freak John came along and interrupted." She snapped her mirror shut and elbowed Haley. "I'm so psyched about the dance! Aren't you?"

"Sure, I guess." Haley probably would have forgotten all about yesterday's announcement of the back-to-school dance as soon as she'd heard it, except that Tracey and Emma had spent the entire lunch period talking about it.

"It's going to be so amazing!" Tracey hugged herself, practically vibrating with excitement. "I need to figure out what I'm going to wear."

Haley blew out a sigh of relief as she finally found her

math book at the bottom of her locker. That answered the foggy question in her mind about whether she'd done the homework—obviously not—but at least she wouldn't have to explain to strict Mr. Washington how she'd forgotten the book.

"Let's get to homeroom," she told Tracey. "I need to do those math problems."

"Okay. Want to copy?" Tracey fell into step as they headed down the hallway.

Haley shook her head. She'd never cheated on an assignment in her life, and she wasn't planning to start now. Besides, Tracey had always been terrible at math. The last thing Haley needed was a bad grade on an assignment, or Aunt Veronica and Uncle Mike might change their minds about letting her do all that extra work to earn money for the clinic.

When Haley and Tracey walked into homeroom, Emma was already in her seat, bent over a magazine. She looked up when Tracey called her name, smiling and peering at her friends through the thick lenses of her glasses. Emma had albinism and was legally blind, which meant she needed those glasses to see well enough to get by. Her funny-looking glasses, white hair, and pale-lavender eyes had made her a target of teasing during elementary school, and occasionally even now. But Haley and Tracey had always stuck by her loyally, and Haley hardly even noticed Emma's differences anymore.

Well, not the differences brought on by her albinism, anyway. Like Tracey, Emma seemed to be developing a strange obsession with clothes, makeup, and boys. Haley wasn't sure which of her friends had gone crazy first, or why they were acting that way all of a sudden. She just hoped they both got over it soon.

"You're finally here!" Emma exclaimed as Haley and Tracey took their seats on either side of her. "I've been dying to talk about the dance. What are we going to wear?"

Tracey squealed and started chattering about dresses and shoes and makeup, but Haley tuned out as she flipped open her math book. She was halfway through the set of problems when Emma poked her on the shoulder.

"Earth to Haley!" Emma said with a giggle. "Did you hear what Trace just said?"

Haley blinked. "No, sorry. What?"

"I said we need to plan a serious shopping trip," Tracey said, leaning past Emma's desk. "I wish we could get down to the city and shop on Michigan Avenue for something really cool. But we might not have time to plan that kind of trip, so I guess we're stuck with the mall."

Emma nodded. "That's okay—I saw some really cute dresses at Finders Keepers last time I was there."

"Ooh, good call. I love that store." Tracey glanced at Haley. "So when do you want to go? How about Friday?"

"Friday?" Haley hesitated, not sure how to respond. She was way too busy to take time out for stuff like shopping or dances. Besides, even if her friends managed to drag her to the dance, there was no way she was wasting any of her hard-earned money on a new dress. Not when she was still counting every penny she earned, hoping it would be enough to pay the clinic fees.

"Yes, Friday." Emma giggled. "You know, it's the day that comes after Thursday? And before Saturday?"

"We really should go then," Tracey urged, pulling a lip gloss out of her purse and slicking it on. "The dance is next

Friday. And we'll need some time to plan our hair and makeup to go with whatever dresses we get."

"I'm not sure I can afford a dress," Haley said. "I'm saving up for that clinic, remember?"

Tracey shrugged. "Just ask your aunt and uncle. They buy the rest of your clothes, right? A dress for the dance is just as important as jeans or whatever."

Not to me, it isn't, Haley thought. *Probably not to Aunt Veronica and Uncle Mike, either.*

Besides, her uncle had just replaced his old tractor and had been grumbling about being in the poorhouse ever since. No way was he going to give Haley money for some stupid dress she'd probably only wear once. No way was she even going to ask him.

She opened her mouth, trying to figure out how to explain that to her friends. The shrill buzz of the bell cut her off before she could say a word.

As the homeroom teacher called for attention, Haley slumped in her seat, relieved.

Saved by the bell, she thought.

◆ CHAPTER ◆
3

AS SHE STEPPED INTO THE BARN ON THURS-
day afternoon, Haley had forgotten all about her friends'
shopping plans. She'd forgotten about the long list of
chores waiting to be completed before dinnertime. She'd
even managed to forget—mostly—about blowing that
English quiz earlier in the day. All she wanted to focus on
right now was Wings.

"Ready for a dressage schooling, Wingsie?" she said
as she clipped the pony into the crossties in the asphalt
aisle of the big, airy old barn. Wings hadn't been happy
about being pulled away from the pile of hay Haley's uncle
had just tossed into the pasture, and as usual, he wasn't

keeping his feelings a secret. He shifted his weight from one foot to another, tossing his head so the clips on the ties jingled against the metal halter rings.

Haley sighed. She knew this mood, and if she'd been planning a cross-country session or even more trot sets, she wouldn't be worried. Wings loved to eat as much as any other horse, but he was easy to distract with something fun. But with dressage on the agenda for that day, she knew it would be an uphill battle. She could only hope that Wings would settle down and focus once he was warmed up.

"I know, buddy," she said as she fetched her grooming bucket from the tack room beside the office, stepping over a cat snoozing in the doorway. "Dressage isn't my favorite phase, either. But it's important, and you know Zina Charles won't be impressed if we rush through every transition and totally forget how to leg-yield."

Dressage was one of the three phases that made up the sport of eventing, the other two being cross-country jumping and show jumping. In the dressage phase, horses and riders had to perform a series of maneuvers and gait changes that tested the horse's training, obedience, and gaits, along with the rider's skill.

Wings raised his head and pranced in place as Bandit dashed into the barn. "You goober," Haley said with a laugh, poking the pony on the shoulder as he almost bumped into her. "It's not like you've never seen a dog before."

She bent to give Bandit a head rub. Then she grabbed a hoofpick out of her bucket.

"Stand still," she ordered Wings. "We're on a tight schedule today."

She was bent over picking out Wings's left front foot when her cell phone rang. Releasing the pony's leg, she straightened up and fished the phone out of her jeans pocket.

"It's me," Tracey's familiar voice said cheerfully when Haley answered. "Just calling to make plans for tomorrow."

"Tomorrow?" Haley pulled the hoofpick out of Wings's reach as he lipped at it, clearly wondering if it was edible. "What's tomorrow?"

"Duh, it's Friday! We're going shopping, remember?"

For a second Haley's mind went blank. Then she

remembered that conversation earlier in the week and cringed as she realized she'd never bothered to follow up on it. Or even think about it again. She'd had more important things on her mind, like reminding Wings during their jump school yesterday that it was possible to jump a flower box without slowing down and trying to grab a bite of the flowers first. Obviously, her friends had taken her silence as a yes.

For a second she was tempted to tell Tracey that she couldn't go. But Tracey could be just as stubborn as Haley herself when she cared about something, and for some unknown reason she seemed to care an awful lot about this stupid dance. Besides, Haley had been so busy lately that she hadn't had much time to hang out with her friends. Maybe a trip to the mall wouldn't be the end of the world. Maybe it would even be fun—sort of, anyway.

"Um, sorry, I sort of forgot about shopping," she told Tracey. "But hang on—let me check."

Setting the hoofpick aside, she scrolled through the calendar app on her phone. She was scheduled to babysit the Vandenberg triplets on Friday evening starting at six o'clock. She didn't get home from school until almost three thirty. Which left plenty of time to work Wings and do her chores before Mr. Vandenberg arrived to pick her up, but not nearly enough to add in even a short trip to the mall, which was a twenty-minute drive away.

"Hales?" Tracey sounded impatient. "You still there?"

"I'm here." Haley pressed the phone to her ear. "Sorry, I don't think I can make it tomorrow."

"What? No!" Tracey exclaimed. "You have to come! We won't have any fun without you."

Haley smiled weakly. "I wish I could. But I'm babysitting tomorrow night, and I really can't skip a day with Wings right now, so close to the clinic."

"Sure you can. Wings is awesome—he's not going to forget how to jump in one day, right?" Tracey laughed. "Come on, you have to come!"

Haley hesitated again, trying to figure out if she could swap out Friday's planned cross-country session with a shorter show jumping school and still make it to the mall and back in time to do stalls. . . .

"No, sorry," she said at last. "It's not going to happen. I'm sure you guys will have fun, though."

There was a moment of silence on the other end of the line. Haley had known Tracey long enough to be pretty sure that she was just mustering her next argument. If she'd given up, she'd already be whining about it.

But Haley's mind was already returning to everything she had to do. Her uncle wanted her to help him dump and scrub the big water tank in the main pasture after her other chores, and she'd barely started her social studies paper—oh, and she couldn't skip the reading for English again or even ditzy Ms. Reyes would probably notice. . . .

"But what are you going to wear, then?" Tracey interrupted her thoughts. "It's not like your closet is overflowing with super-stylish choices."

"I'll just have to wear something I already have," Haley said, picking a stray bit of hay out of Wings's mane. "I've still got time to figure it out, right? When's the dance again?"

Tracey's loud sigh carried through the phone, telling Haley more clearly than words that her friend considered

her a hopeless cause. "Next Friday," Tracey said. "As in one week from tomorrow."

"Next Friday?" Haley pulled up the calendar app again. When she scrolled down to the following weekend, her heart sank. She had a dressage lesson scheduled with her local trainer next Saturday—Jan had even agreed to come to Haley's place to teach her, since Uncle Mike couldn't haul Wings to her farm that day. Haley was grateful to the busy trainer for rearranging her schedule that way, and she wanted to show it. She'd been planning to give Wings a bath on Friday night so his white parts sparkled for the lesson, and maybe give her tack a good cleaning as well if there was time.

"Hello?" Tracey said. "Are you there?"

"I'm here. I was just looking at my calendar. Um, I don't think I can make the dance."

"What?"

Haley winced as her friend's shriek rang through the barn. Even Wings pricked his ears and looked at the phone.

"Sorry," Haley said. "My trainer is coming out early that Saturday morning and I have a ton to do to get ready."

"Can't you reschedule?" Tracey said. "Maybe she can

come later in the day, or on Sunday. Or the weekend after."

"The weekend after is the Zina Charles clinic." Haley tried to stay patient. Okay, so she'd probably mentioned the date of the clinic about a thousand times. She couldn't really be mad at Tracey for forgetting, though. After all, she herself couldn't seem to keep that stupid school dance in her head for more than five minutes. Not that it was the same kind of thing at all . . .

"I can't believe this!" Tracey sounded genuinely upset. "Seriously, Hales, you're going to regret it if you miss all your important middle school moments because you're riding or whatever. This is the first dance of the year! What's Owen going to think if you don't show?"

Haley couldn't care less what Owen thought. But she didn't bother to say so.

"I'm sorry," she said instead. "I'll make the next dance—promise."

"But that'll be months away!" Tracey sounded horrified. "Look, I swear I won't even try to convince you to go out with Ems and me afterward. The dance ends at nine thirty, so you could be home in bed by ten."

For a second Haley considered that. Maybe she could tell the boys they'd have to do their own chores that day. If she rushed straight home from school, she just might be able to fit in her planned schooling with Wings, then still have time to give him a bath and do her own chores before the dance. Jan probably wouldn't even notice the condition of her tack. . . .

Haley shook her head. Why was she trying so hard to figure out a way to rework her schedule to fit in a dance she had no interest in attending in the first place? Since when did she compromise something she cared about for something she didn't? Okay, so if things were different, if she had more spare time, getting all dressed up and going to the dance with her friends might not be so bad. It might even be fun. But she didn't have time right now, and that was that.

She opened her mouth to tell Tracey that, then thought better of it when Wings tossed his head and pawed. There was no time to get into a long, drawn-out argument with Tracey right now.

"I'll see how it's going next week and decide then, okay?" Haley said hurriedly. "Look, I have to go—my aunt is calling me."

"Okay." Tracey sounded hopeful, and Haley knew she'd be hearing more about that dance, probably much sooner than she wanted to.

But she wasn't going to think about that right now.

"Come on, Wings," she said, grabbing a brush out of her grooming bucket. "Let's go do some dressage."

By the time she crawled into bed that night, Haley could hardly keep her eyes open. Stifling a yawn, she grabbed her laptop and opened it as she snuggled back against her pillows. Moment later she was logging on to the Pony Post.

She smiled when she saw Maddie's latest entry:

[MADDIE] PAGING HALEY! How's it going? Did you and the Wingman have a good dressage school today? What are u working on w/him tomorrow?

Haley was still smiling as she opened a text box to respond. It was nice to have friends who understood what was really important to her. Her smile faded slightly as her mind flashed to Tracey and Emma. Once upon a time, they'd both been that kind of friend too. Okay, so neither of them was super-interested in horses—Tracey occasionally went trail riding with her cousins up in Door County and usually ended up complaining about her sore muscles afterward, while Ems was nervous around any animal larger than a golden retriever. But both of them had come and cheered Haley and Wings on in their very first competition together, along with most of those since. And they'd both loved hearing about Haley's big plans to move up the levels, maybe even make training and riding and competing her life's work someday.

"That was then, this is now," Haley muttered under her breath.

Then she turned her attention back to the Pony Post. She typed her response quickly:

[HALEY] Dressage today was good, mostly. W. was kinda up at first, but I let him canter around the ring about eleventy-billion times to warm up, and he settled down after that. Still have stuff to work on in our dr. lesson next week, tho!

It was only a few seconds after she hit send that another line popped up beneath hers.

[NINA] Haley! You're here! I'm on right now too.

Haley's smile returned. Most of the time, the Pony Posters had to wait for responses to their posts to one another. After all, they were spread out across three different time zones. Just about the only times they were all on the site together were birthdays and other special occasions. But once in a while, two or even three of them would happen to be logged on at the same time so they could have a real-time conversation.

[HALEY] I'm here! Just barely—
had a looooong day today!

[NINA] I bet! The clinic is almost here, huh?

[HALEY] Tell me about it! I'd be too excited to
breathe if I wasn't too busy to breathe! LOL!

[NINA] ha-ha! Maybe that's good—u won't get so nervous about riding in front of a superstar that way.

As she read Nina's message, Haley yawned so widely it felt as if her face might crack in two. Glancing at the clock, she did some quick mental math. Just six and a half hours until her alarm went off. Tomorrow was going to be another long day—even without a trip to the mall in the mix.

[HALEY] U may be right. Anyway, I'd better go—falling asleep on keyboard! LOL! Sorry I'm not more chatty 2night!

[NINA] No worries, I get it. Go get some sleep, girl. & keep us posted!

[HALEY] U know I will! G'night!

• CHAPTER •

4

"I'M HOME!" HALEY SHOUTED AS SHE RUSHED through the front door, barely pausing to toss her jacket in the general direction of the closet. She was already mentally adding up the minutes and seconds it would take to tack up Wings, ride out to the cross-country field and school him over a few jumps, cool him out, do her chores, then get back into the house in time to throw on something clean before Mr. Vandenberg showed up.

"Haley." Aunt Veronica appeared in the kitchen doorway when Haley was halfway up the stairs. "Stop."

Aunt Veronica was a petite, slightly plump woman with rosy cheeks and an angelic smile. But her softness was backed with steel. When she gave an order, even her tough old farmer husband always obeyed instantly.

Haley stopped with one foot halfway to the next step. "Yes?"

"Mrs. Vandenberg called." Aunt Veronica wiped her hands on the dishrag she was holding. She almost never stopped moving—if she wasn't in her home office working as a freelance computer programmer, she was cleaning or cooking or weeding the garden. "One of the kids has a fever, so they're staying in tonight. They won't need you after all."

Haley just stood there as her mind struggled to take in this turn of events. "Oh," she said at last. "No babysitting tonight?"

"No babysitting tonight." Her aunt shrugged. "She sent her apologies and said they'll probably reschedule their dinner, and they'll call you then."

"Okay." Haley wasn't sure what to do for a moment. She'd been counting on the money from tonight. If the Vandenbergs didn't call her back before the clinic, she'd have trouble making up the difference.

But at least there was a silver lining. Now she had some extra time this afternoon. It was tempting to ask Jake and Danny if they wanted her to do their chores today after all. But then she had a better idea.

"Tracey and Emma wanted me to go shopping with them today," she told her aunt. "Is that okay?"

Aunt Veronica looked surprised. "Of course," she said immediately. "You've been working so hard lately, it'll be good for you to get out and have some fun with your friends." She stepped over and smoothed down Haley's hair. "I'm really sorry your uncle and I can't help you out more with the cost of your clinic. You've certainly earned it with your devotion to that rotten little pony of yours."

Haley laughed. Ever since she'd sprained her wrist last year hitting the ground after an extra-exuberant buck, Wings had been officially known to her aunt as "that rotten pony." But Haley knew Aunt Veronica didn't mean it. For one thing, she always smiled when she said it. For another, talking about Wings often sent her aunt off on endless stories about her own "rotten pony" from her childhood, a mischievous little Appaloosa mare with a habit of scraping off her riders on any available tree or fence post. But that mare had made Aunt Veronica a terrific rider, even if she didn't have much time for it anymore. And it was Aunt Veronica who'd convinced Uncle Mike that Wings would do the same for Haley.

"Okay, thanks," Haley said, pulling out her phone. "I'd better call before they leave without me."

"Ta-da!" Tracey leaped out of the dressing-room stall and struck a pose. She'd traded her jeans and T-shirt for a cream-colored lace baby-doll dress. "What do you think? Is it totally me?"

Haley smiled weakly from her seat on a bench near the three-way mirror. The dress was way too short and tight—there was no way Tracey's strict father would let her leave the house in it. But she suspected that wasn't the response Tracey was looking for.

Meanwhile Emma peeked out of the next stall. "Let me see!" She poked her glasses back up her nose. "Whoa, you look gorgeous, Trace!"

"Thanks." Tracey twirled and giggled. "Do you think Nick would agree?"

Emma giggled too. "He thinks you look gorgeous in gym shorts," she said. "He'll die if you show up at the dance in that!"

"So, what do you think, Hales?" Tracey stepped over in front of Haley. "Is it me?"

"Um . . ." Haley shrugged. "I don't know. I think I liked the blue one better."

"Which blue one?" Tracey glanced into her dressing room, which was crammed with at least half a dozen dresses. "The one with the sequins, or the one with the full skirt?"

"Don't forget the one from the last store," Emma put in. "Remember? With the chiffon? I thought you looked amazing in that one."

Haley stifled a yawn as the two of them started chattering about the relative merits of the three blue dresses. So far, this shopping trip hadn't been much fun. Still, she told herself that keeping her friends happy was worth a few hours of boredom. She'd still have plenty of time to school Wings when she got home, and Aunt Veronica had even offered to set the table for her so she wouldn't have to cut the ride short.

Besides, I could tell Tracey was really happy I changed my mind about today, Haley reminded herself. *Maybe now she won't be as mad when I tell her I really can't make the dance next Friday.*

Because the more she thought about it, the more certain she was that she couldn't fit in the dance. Not if it might mess up Saturday's lesson. Her last couple of dressage schoolings had reminded her of several things she wanted to ask Jan to help her with before the clinic, and she needed to be wide awake and ready to focus. After all, this was important. She and Wings definitely didn't want to embarrass themselves in front of Zina Charles!

If they actually made it to the clinic, that was. There was still a ton to do before then, including figuring out how to make up for today's lost babysitting money. Haley also wanted to find time to polish her tall boots, and oil her jumping saddle, and clip Wings's muzzle and fetlocks, and . . .

She blinked as she realized Tracey was waving a

hand in her face. "Wake up!" Tracey said. "You're totally spacing out!"

"Sorry." Haley blinked and straightened up. "Um, what were you saying?"

Emma popped out of her dressing room, wearing a cute pale-pink dress with a full skirt. "She was saying you need to try on some dresses already. How do I look?"

"Adorable!" Tracey exclaimed, hurrying over and tweaking the sleeve of Emma's dress. "That color is perfect on you."

Emma grimaced. "Thank goodness. I looked like a ghost in that red one!"

"No, you didn't," Tracey said loyally. "But this one's definitely better. Don't you think so, Hales?"

"Sure," Haley agreed. "I like it."

"Good. It's definitely on the list." Emma surveyed herself in the mirror, turning this way and that to check out all the angles. "Anyway, that red dress might look better on one of you. Why don't you try it, Haley?"

"Um, I don't know." Haley shrugged. "I really don't want to spend any money on a new dress."

Tracey poked her on the shoulder. "So what? That doesn't mean you can't have fun trying some on."

Wiggling into one scratchy, uncomfortable, too-girly dress after another wasn't Haley's idea of fun, but she didn't bother to say so. Shouldn't her best friends already know that? After all, until recently *they* hadn't liked that kind of thing either.

"Okay," she said. "But I don't think the dresses at this store are really my style. I'll wait for the next one."

Tracey and Emma traded a look. "That's what you said at the last store," Tracey said. "But whatever, we're going to Finders Keepers next. I bet we can find you something cute there."

"True. That place really is more Haley's style," Emma said, heading for her dressing room. "Come on, let's get changed and head over there."

Ten minutes later, Haley trailed behind her friends as they hurried down the mall aisle. She sneaked a peek at her watch and was surprised to discover that they'd only been shopping for a little over an hour. It felt more like a day and a half!

She immediately felt guilty for thinking that. Okay, so maybe Tracey and Emma were acting as if they'd been abducted by aliens and replaced with shopping-obsessed pod people. They were still her best friends. Maybe Haley just needed to relax and stop worrying about all the other things she could be doing right now. She should at least *try* to have fun, right? Especially since she might not have another chance to hang out with her friends outside of school until after the clinic.

"Is anyone else getting hungry?" she asked, hoping to distract the others from their dress-seeking mission. "I was in such a rush to meet you guys that I didn't get an after-school snack."

"Me!" Emma rubbed her stomach. "Let's go to the Mexican place—I love their milk shakes."

The mall's food court was crowded, as it almost always was on Friday afternoons. Haley spotted Jake goofing off with some of his high school friends over by the ice cream place, and she recognized several other kids from around town as well.

Wow, I guess Tracey and Ems aren't the only ones who

like to come here, Haley thought with a flicker of surprise. She hadn't really imagined that everyone she knew rushed home to clean stalls and ride horses after school. But somehow, she hadn't thought much about what they might be doing instead, either.

She and her friends wound their way through the crowd to the taco stand and got in line. As they waited, Haley studied the menu.

"I think I'll just have an iced tea," she said, digging into her pocket for the leftover change from lunch.

"What? I thought you were hungry," Emma said.

"I was," Haley said. "I mean I am, sort of. But I don't want to ruin my appetite so close to dinner."

Emma blinked behind her thick glasses, her pale eyes confused. "But I thought you said you were going riding after this," she said.

Tracey shrugged. "Actually, I was thinking about ordering the large nacho platter, but I'm not sure I can eat it all," she said. "Want to share, Hales? My treat."

Haley shot her a look. She suspected that Tracey had guessed the real reason Haley didn't want to order any food. Namely, she didn't want to spend any of her hard-earned money. The cost of those nachos could make the difference between making it to the clinic and coming up a few dollars short.

Normally Haley wouldn't have accepted Tracey's offer without insisting on paying for her half. She didn't need charity from anyone, even her best friend. But her stomach was grumbling, and she still had a lot to do before dinner.

"Sure, thanks," she said. "I'll get it next time, okay?"

"Whatever." Tracey flashed her a smile, then hurried forward to order, waving away the money Haley tried to hand her for the iced tea.

Soon they had their food. Haley glanced around as they stepped away from the counter.

"It's pretty packed in here," she said. "I don't even see a free table. Maybe we should go down the aisle and find a bench instead."

"No, let's stay here," Tracey said quickly. "I think I see a table over there."

She hurried toward a tiny table shoved up against the

back of a waste bin. Haley shrugged and followed. Soon the three of them were crowded around the rickety table.

Emma slurped her milk shake. "So Haley," she said as she licked off her chocolate mustache. "When's that horse clinic thing of yours again?"

"Two weeks from tomorrow," Haley replied. "I can't wait!"

Tracey reached for a nacho. "Okay, so after that you'll be back to normal, right?" She giggled. "I mean, as normal as you ever get. As in, not always having to rush off to ride or do extra chores every second of the day."

"I guess so." Haley hadn't really thought about how her friends might see her behavior over the past couple of months. Had she really been that busy? "I mean, I'll definitely want to give Wings some time off," she added. "He's been working really hard too, and . . ."

She let her words trail off. Tracey obviously wasn't listening anymore. She was staring at something over Haley's right shoulder.

Glancing that way, Haley saw that a group of rowdy boys their age had just entered the food court. There were four of them, all dressed in matching soccer shirts. They were shoving and laughing their way toward the burger place.

"Look, it's Nick!" Emma hissed, her eyes bright with interest as she glanced at Tracey.

Tracey ran a hand over her hair. "Duh, I see him," she hissed back. "Do I look okay? Anything in my teeth?"

Haley didn't know why Tracey was so worried about it. Nick Jankowski wasn't even looking in their direction.

"Are you going to go talk to him?" she asked.

"What?" Tracey let out a short, breathless yelp of laughter. "No way! But maybe he'll come over here."

"Do you think he'll ask you to the dance?" Emma asked.

Tracey shrugged, her eyes never leaving Nick and his friends. "Probably not," she said. "He's super-shy. But he might ask me to dance once we're there."

"Or you could ask him," Haley said. "*You're* not exactly shy."

Tracey giggled. "What do you mean? I'm totally shy!"

"Yeah, right!" Emma let out a snort.

"Well, this is different." Tracey shot Nick another look, then leaned across the table. "But listen, that reminds me. My mom said she'd talk to my dad about maybe letting me have a boy-girl party soon! Isn't that cool?"

Emma gasped. "Really? That would be so cool!" She elbowed Haley so hard she almost spit out a mouthful of half-chewed nacho. "Did you hear that, Hales?"

"I heard." Haley didn't know what the big deal was. Back in elementary school, boys and girls had invited one another to their birthday parties all the time. She wasn't quite sure when that had changed. Come to think of it, nobody really had birthday parties much anymore. Haley hadn't really missed them, since she was usually busy with Wings on the weekend anyway.

"So when is it going to be?" Emma asked. "Your birthday?"

Tracey waved a hand. "I don't want to wait that long! I don't know, though. It depends what my dad says. But I'm thinking it'll be on a Saturday, so we'll have plenty of time to get ready. If it's not too cold yet, we can have it out on the deck and hook up my sister's speakers so we can dance, and . . ."

There was more, but Haley stopped listening. She wasn't that interested in some big boy-girl party, especially one with dancing. Besides, she had way too many other, more important things to worry about.

Shoving another nacho in her mouth, she started running through Wings's training schedule in her head while her friends chattered on.

✦ CHAPTER ✦
5

THE NEXT SEVERAL DAYS PASSED IN A BLUR.
On Tuesday after school, Haley stopped in the kitchen
just long enough to grab a granola bar. She unwrapped it,
shoved half of it in her mouth, and grabbed her boots from
the mat by the back door.

As she pulled on one of the boots, her aunt poked
her head out of her office, which adjoined the mudroom.
"You're still going to help me plant those bulbs today,
right, Haley?" Aunt Veronica said. "Or don't you have
time after all?"

Haley blinked. She'd totally forgotten! That morning
at breakfast, her aunt had mentioned wanting to plant the

flower bulbs she'd brought home from her garden club plant exchange to spruce up the yard. She'd offered Haley some cash if she helped. It wasn't enough to make up for the missed babysitting job, but it was a start.

"No, it's fine," Haley said. "I still want to do it. I can ride afterward."

Two hours later, the job was finally done. Haley had dirt under her fingernails, and her shoulders ached from shoving the ancient steel bulb planter into the hard, dry ground over and over again. Kicking off the garden clogs she'd borrowed from her aunt, Haley quickly pulled on her paddock boots and hurried outside.

When she entered the barn, she was surprised to find all three of the family's quarter horses standing in the aisle. Rusty and Jet were in the crossties, while Chico stood ground-tied nearby, his sleepy, blocky head hanging low and his tail swishing lazily at flies. Wings was in his stall, peering out over the half door. Jake and Danny were there too. Jake was running a brush over Rusty's broad back, while Danny was with Chico, tightening the cinch on Uncle Mike's big old hand-tooled Western saddle.

"Are you going riding today?" Haley asked, bending to pet Bandit as the dog raced over to greet her.

Danny rolled his eyes at her. While everyone said Jake was the spitting image of Uncle Mike, Danny took after his mother. Like Aunt Veronica, he was small and quick and always moving.

"Duh," he said, giving Chico's cinch another tug. "You really are lost in your own little English riding world these days, aren't you?"

Jake grinned at Haley over his horse's back. "Yeah. She's walking around with dreams of prancing and jumping taking up her entire brain," he drawled. "She doesn't have time for boring stuff like helping us clear around the sugar maples."

"Oh right, that's today, isn't it?" Haley felt a pang of wistfulness. She'd always loved everything about the family tradition of maple syruping. There were numerous mature sugar maples on their property and those of several neighboring farms, and every fall Haley, her cousins, and her uncle went out to clear the brush and vines that had grown up around them over the summer. That would make it easier in the winter, when they returned to tap the trees. Clearing the brush was hard, hot, scratchy work, but it was fun, too. The four of them always saddled up and rode out, winding their way through the woods and singing old songs that Uncle Mike had learned from his father and grandfather.

"I can't believe Pop's letting you get away with skipping out on us," Danny grumbled, hurrying over and grabbing his saddle off the rack in the tack room. "That'll be more work for the rest of us."

"She probably doesn't want to get her hands dirty," Jake told him with a smirk. "You know how those English riders are, with their white gloves and their spotless boots and stuff."

Danny snorted with laughter as he swung the saddle onto Jet's back. "Yeah. Still, if she doesn't help us make the syrup, I say she doesn't get to eat it either. Mom and Pop should make her eat her pancakes plain until she starts helping again."

"Whatever," Haley muttered, heading over to Wings's stall. She wasn't in the mood for the boys' teasing today.

For one thing, she really did wish she could go with them to clear brush. It didn't seem fair that it just happened to be time for that particular task right now, right when she was too busy to go.

But it was what it was. Haley was sure that Zina Charles had probably missed a fun outing or two on her way to the top. And if she could do it, Haley could too. She wanted to be the best, just like Zina. And being the best meant making sacrifices. Besides, the boys were just goofing around—they didn't really need her help today, and they knew it.

"Are you guys almost done with the crossties?" she asked as she led Wings out of the stall.

The pony was on his toes, ears pricked at his herd mates as he jostled into Haley. She stuck an elbow into his chest to back him off. It was no surprise that he was full of energy today. Haley always gave him Mondays off. She'd read online that a lot of the big, professional barns did that, and it seemed like a good idea to her. It gave Wings a chance to rest, hang out, and just be a horse one day a week—no riding, no grooming, just eating and napping and doing his own thing out in the pasture.

Too bad nobody gives me a day off like that, Haley thought ruefully, flashing from the bulb planting she'd just finished to the barn chores waiting for her after her ride to the homework she'd have to fit in sometime between dinner, house chores, and sleep.

"I'm done." Jake slipped the bit into Rusty's mouth and led him forward, leaving him standing beside Chico with the reins draped over his neck. "All yours."

"Thanks." Haley clipped Wings into the ties. He immediately took a step backward, putting pressure on his halter and almost stepping on Haley's foot in the process. "Watch it, Wings!" she said, giving him a sharp poke on the shoulder. He swung away so fast his rump bumped into the wall with a thump that made even Chico lift his head slightly in surprise.

"Wings is such a dork," Danny commented. "When are you going to sell him and get a real horse?" He gave Jet a pat on the shoulder.

"Sell him?" Jake let out a snort. "Who'd pay good money for that funny-looking little spotted thing? She'd be lucky to give him away."

It was far from the first time the boys had made that sort of joke. But today Haley wasn't finding their stand-up routine particularly funny.

"Wings is worth all three of your horses put together," she snapped. "If you tried to get Rusty or Jet to jump a crossrail, they'd probably trip over it. Or if you made them do a dressage test, they'd faint halfway through."

"Whatever, Haley." Danny whistled to Bandit, who was sniffing at something on the floor behind Wings. "Yo, mutt, watch yourself. You barely have a brain as it is; you don't want Haley's nutty pony to kick the rest of it out of your head."

Gritting her teeth, Haley willed herself not to respond. She knew she was cranky from rushing around with too much to do on too little sleep, and she also knew she had to get over it. Wings could feel her mood and was likely to take offense if Haley was lacking in her usual sense of humor. And they couldn't afford a bad ride today. Not with the Zina Charles clinic only a week and a half away.

Haley took a deep breath and closed her eyes, focusing on why she was doing this. The clinic. She pictured herself riding in front of Zina, soaking up the pro rider's knowledge, experience, and enthusiasm, and soon she felt calmer. *That* was why she was doing this. She had to remember that, and everything would be all right.

"Okay, boy." She opened her eyes and gave Wings a pat. "Let's settle down and get to work, okay?"

By the time she finished grooming and saddling the pony, Uncle Mike had arrived. "Thanks for tacking up for me, boys," he said, waking Chico up with a hearty pat on the neck. "Things were busy at the pharmacy today—I thought I'd never get out of there!"

Uncle Mike was first and foremost a farmer. He'd been born on this very farm, along with his younger brother, Haley's father. But over the years, bits of the property had been sold off to help pay the mortgage, as had the dairy herd and various equipment. These days the farm still made money, mostly in hay, organic vegetables, hunting leases, and the occasional sale of a side of grass-fed beef.

But Uncle Mike also worked part-time as a pharmacist at one of the drugstores in town to help make ends meet.

"No problem, Pop." Jake patted the bulging saddlebags he'd attached to his horse. "Tools are ready too."

Uncle Mike rubbed his horse's nose, then gave a tug on the reins to lead him outside. "Good, good. Come on, Chico, let's roll. Shake a leg, Haley—get that pony bridled and let's go!"

"She's not coming, remember?" Danny said. "She's got some important horse prancing to do today instead."

"Oh, right." Uncle Mike's mustache twitched as he glanced at Haley. "Almost forgot. Won't be the same without you there, Haley. But have fun."

"Thanks." Haley waited until they'd all gone, listening for the creak of the big gate leading into the main pasture. From there, the riders would cut across to the woods, winding their way down and across the brook. Haley had ridden that trail so many times she could see every rock and tree root in her mind's eye.

For a second she was tempted to call out for them to wait for her. Sure, they'd make fun of her riding along in her English saddle. But teasing and goofing around was just part of the fun. . . .

"We can't," she said aloud, causing Bandit to prick his ears and stare at her. She sighed. "We really can't. Anyway, we'll have fun too, won't we, Wingsie?"

She slipped on the bridle and led Wings out of the barn, turning in the opposite direction from the way the others had gone. Today was scheduled to be a conditioning ride, and Haley was planning to trot and canter up and down the hills of the neighbors' property, where she had standing permission to ride whenever she liked. Getting there meant walking along the highway for about four hundred yards until she was past the perimeter fence and could cut through another neighbor's fallow cornfield. There was a wide, grassy shoulder the whole way, but it still made Haley's aunt and uncle nervous to think of her riding beside such a busy road on her rather unpredictable pony. When she'd first proposed the route, they'd made her promise to walk Wings in hand until they got to the cornfield, and Haley knew better than to let them catch her doing otherwise.

Bandit and one of the other dogs, an amiable but lazy yellow Lab, were at her heels as she crossed the yard. "Stay back, you two," Haley ordered as she reached the gate. "Sorry, you can't tag along today. You're not allowed out by the road."

The Lab backed off, but Bandit let out an eager bark and crowded forward as Haley reached for the latch. His lean body pressed against the gate, making Wings prance and stare down at him with suspicion.

"Bandit, no!" Haley said, a bit of her earlier impatience creeping back as she nudged at the dog with her foot. He dodged her, trying to wedge himself into the inch-wide opening between gate and fence.

Haley blew out a sigh of frustration. Couldn't anything go smoothly today?

Chill, she thought. *He's just a dog; he doesn't understand.*

"Bandit, sit," she ordered firmly.

The dog turned and stared at her. Then, slowly, his haunches sank to the ground.

"Good boy," Haley said. Casting a glance around the area, she spotted a crooked twig lying in the dust.

Grabbing it, she hurled it back into the barnyard as far as she could. "Fetch!" she cried.

Bandit barked and leaped into action, chasing the stick. Haley quickly swung the gate open, glad that Wings wasn't the slow, lazy type like the quarter horses. By the time Bandit noticed what was going on, girl and pony were through and the gate safely latched once again.

"Sorry, boy," Haley said as the dog raced over and whined at her from his side of the gate. "See you when we get back."

Fifteen minutes later she was in the saddle, trotting across the barren cornfield. Wings was alert, his ears swiveling every which way as birds whirled in the blue sky overhead and a small herd of deer bounded out of their path, heading for the safety of the woods. Haley breathed in deeply. The air was warm and smelled of dirt and pine, the summer and winter scents mingling in a way that reminded her of everything good about both seasons. Wings let out a snort and she smiled, suddenly not wanting to be anywhere else except right here, right now.

All her worries suddenly seemed much less

important—the chores waiting for her back home, her boy-obsessed friends, even the missed ride with her family. This was why she did this—this feeling. Just her and her pony, feeling good, ready to take on the world.

"That was fun, huh?" Haley gave Wings a scratch on the withers. They were crossing the cornfield again, this time heading for home after a good ride. She hadn't thought about anything except enjoying her pony and making sure they did what they needed to do.

Just then Haley felt a weird little movement against her seat. For a second she thought it was Wings trying to shudder off a fly or something. But then she realized it was her phone vibrating in her back pocket. She almost ignored it but knew her aunt would worry if it was her calling and Haley didn't answer.

"Hello?" Haley said without checking to see who it was.

"Hales? Hi, it's me!" Tracey sounded excited. "Guess what?"

"What?" Haley nudged Wings with her left heel, steering him around a rut in the field.

"My dad said yes!" Tracey squealed. "Can you believe it? He actually said yes!"

Haley blinked. "Um, what?"

"The party!" Tracey sounded impatient now. "Seriously, keep up, Hales! We've only been talking about it all week, right?"

Now Haley caught on. It was true—ever since that day at the mall, the only time Tracey and Emma weren't talking obsessively about the coming dance was when they switched the topic to Tracey's boy-girl party.

"Oh," she said. "Um, that's cool. So when's the party?"

"That's the best part," Tracey said. "It's Saturday night—as in *this* Saturday night, the day after the dance. Isn't that perfect?"

Haley pulled Wings to an abrupt halt, not sure if she'd heard her friend right. "This Saturday night?" she echoed. "You're having a party this Saturday night? As in, four days from now?"

"Uh-huh." Tracey let out a little squeal of happiness. "Like I said, perfect! It'll be like one big super-romantic fun weekend, you know?"

Haley's heart sank. She might be able to skip out on a school dance, but Tracey would never forgive her if she missed her very first boy-girl party.

"Um, isn't that kind of late notice?" Haley said. "I mean, some people might already have plans or whatever. Plus, people's parents might not let them go out two nights in a row. Are you sure it wouldn't be better to wait a few weeks?"

Like, until after my clinic, when I might have enough time to breathe, let alone go to a party? she added silently.

"No, seriously, it'll be fine. I don't want to give my dad time to change his mind." Tracey giggled. "Besides, I happen to know that Nick Jankowski is free that night, and really, that's all that matters, right? Oh! And of course Owen will be there too."

Haley glanced down as Wings took a step to the side, clearly tired of standing still. She nudged him into a walk.

"Okay," she said slowly. "Look, I'm riding right now, so I should go. Call you later?"

"Sure." Tracey sounded distracted. "I need to go too—

Mom's taking me shopping for food and stuff. Wow, there's so much to do!"

"Tell me about it," Haley muttered as she hung up.

Then she just sat there, riding along with her reins slack, staring into space as she tried to figure out exactly how she was supposed to cram one more thing into her already packed-to-the-gills schedule.

• CHAPTER •

6

THAT NIGHT HALEY WAS SO EXHAUSTED SHE
could barely make it up the stairs to her bedroom. She peeled
off her clothes, dropping them in a pile by the door. Taking
them to the hamper in the hall would have to wait until morning.

As she pulled on her nightgown, she noticed her laptop sitting at the foot of her bed with her school bag. That
reminded her—she hadn't posted on the Pony Post in a
couple of days.

She crawled into bed with the computer and pulled up
the site. Even as tired as she was, her friends' latest entries
made her smile and feel a little more alert.

[BROOKE] Hi Haley! Check in when u can and let us know how it's going!

[NINA] Don't harass her, lol! She's prolly too busy riding every second of the day so she can rly wow ZC next w/e. U can do it, girl!

[MADDIE] Jealous! Wish I could ride every day!! But I'll just have to live thru u, Haley! Gogogo Haley go!

[BROOKE] lol, ur a good cheerleader, M.

[NINA] Ya, Haley, wish we could all be there to cheer you and Wingsie on in person for the clinic!

[BROOKE] And to help u earn $ for it too. Maddie is a pro at crazy ways to make $, right?

[MADDIE] lol, too true!

Haley's smile widened at that. Over the summer, Maddie had feared that "her" Chincoteague pony was about to be sold. Cloudy didn't actually belong to Maddie—she was a lesson horse at a local barn. But Maddie loved her just as much as if she owned her, so she'd tried to raise enough cash to buy her. Luckily, the owner had decided not to sell after all. That was a good thing, since Maddie had failed to clear her plan with her parents, who had no interest in owning a pony!

Still, Haley agreed with Nina and the other Pony Posters—she wished they were close enough to do more than cheer her on long distance too. If she took Maddie's energy and optimistic outlook, Nina's creativity and confidence, and Brooke's loyalty and thoughtfulness and combined them with her own work ethic and determination, how could she fail? Besides, it would be nice to have her friends right there to cheer her on. Friends who understood why she was doing this.

For a moment her mind wandered to Tracey and Emma. Instead of helping, it felt as if they—especially

Tracey—were making Haley's life more difficult.

But she shook off those thoughts. That wasn't fair. How could she expect them to understand? Both of them had plenty of hobbies and interests of their own, but neither had the kind of passion for anything that Haley did for eventing. Well, except maybe lately for boys and shopping and makeup . . .

Pushing that thought aside too, Haley glanced over the remaining Pony Post entries.

> [BROOKE] Anyway, H, let us know
> how it's going when u have time.

> [NINA] Ya, esp. let us know about the $.
> But you're def. going to make it, right?

Haley yawned as she tried to figure out how to respond to Nina's question. Was she going to make it?

She rolled over and opened the drawer in her bedside table, pulling out the envelope where she was keeping her babysitting cash. Her aunt and uncle were keeping tabs on what the boys owed her and would make sure she got paid before the clinic.

Opening the calculator on her laptop, Haley added up the two numbers, then added in the paltry amount left in her savings account, where her grandparents deposited birthday and Christmas money. If only she hadn't spent so much on those new rubber reins a few months ago! Her old ones probably would have held up for another year. But it was way too late to return them now. Haley chewed her lower lip as she studied the total on the calculator.

Still not enough, she thought with a flash of panic.

Leaning back against her pillows, she thought over her schedule for the next ten days. She was babysitting a neighbor's toddler after school on Thursday, and one of her uncle's coworkers had hired her to clean out his henhouse on Friday afternoon. Oh, and she couldn't forget about the Tompkinses—they'd asked her to water their plants and feed the cat this weekend while they were down in Chicago visiting family. They always tipped her in addition to the agreed-on amount, so that was an extra few dollars. . . .

Haley's head swam as she tried to remember what else she was doing. There were more chores for her cousins, of course, and the Vandenbergs might call again before the clinic, though she knew she couldn't count on that. She added the other numbers in with the one on the calculator. Then she deleted everything and started again, making sure she entered each amount correctly.

Finally she smiled. She returned the cash to its drawer, glancing up at the clinic flyer on her bulletin board as she did so. Then she opened a new text box.

[HALEY] Hi all! Thx for the cheers & stuff! I don't wanna jinx anything, but I think I can do it. I just figured it all out, & by the end of next wk I should have enough to pay the balance of the clinic fees, plus a lil extra $ to put diesel in Uncle M's truck to haul us there.

She knew it was way too late for any of her friends to be on the site at the moment, so she clicked off as soon as she'd sent the response. Setting the laptop aside, she snuggled into bed, feeling hopeful as she drifted off to sleep.

"See you this afternoon," Haley told Wings as she turned him out in the pasture. It was Wednesday morning, and she'd decided to put off that day's trot sets until after school. The Vandenbergs still hadn't called about babysitting, and skipping her morning ride had allowed Haley to finish all her chores, so she didn't have anything to do that afternoon except spend time with Wings. Well, that and her usual afternoon chores, of course. But that should still give her plenty of time to get those trot sets done, and maybe pull the pony's thick, unruly mane. Their next dressage school could wait until the next day. Then they'd do another jumping session on Friday to freshen him up for Saturday's lesson.

Wings snuffled at her hand, letting out a snort as he smelled the mint she was holding. Haley laughed and turned her palm up, letting the pony snarf up the treat. Then, after one last pat, she headed for the house.

"Haley!" Aunt Veronica paused halfway to the table

with a platter of scrambled eggs, looking surprised. "You're in early this morning."

Uncle Mike peered at Haley over the top of the local farming paper. "Does this mean you actually have time for a real breakfast today?"

"Uh-huh." Haley slid into her seat beside Danny. She checked her watch. Still almost half an hour until it would be time to leave for school. "Please pass the milk."

Her aunt set the platter in front of her. "I have to admit, we were starting to worry that you were spreading yourself too thin," she said. "But it seems your time management skills are improving."

"Thanks," Haley said as she helped herself to some eggs. "I think I am getting a little better at this."

Jake snorted. "Watch it with the compliments, Mom. Haley already thinks she's headed for the Olympics any day now."

"Yeah." Danny laughed. "Too bad there's no Olympic event for stinky feet! She'd win that one for sure."

"Only if you didn't enter," Haley shot back.

Her uncle grinned. "All right, enough talk of stinky

feet at the breakfast table. You're going to make me lose my appetite."

Aunt Veronica patted him on the shoulder as she bustled by on her way back to the stove. "No worries, kids. That'll never happen."

Haley laughed along with her cousins, then settled down to enjoying her first real family breakfast in what felt like forever.

Haley was humming under her breath as she entered homeroom. She was still in a good mood after her relatively easy morning, and it was nice to feel full after breakfast instead of getting by on half a piece of toast or a quick gulp of orange juice. She glanced around the room. Tracey hadn't shown up at Haley's locker, and she wasn't at her desk, either, though Emma was in her usual seat.

"Where's Trace?" Haley asked as she dumped her backpack on the floor and sat down.

"Not sure." Emma looked up from her social studies book, blinking at Haley from behind her glasses. "She's been super-busy ever since her dad said yes to the party."

She sat up straighter and smiled. "Speaking of the party, are you totally psyched?"

"Sure, I guess."

Just like that, Haley felt her happy mood slowly seeping out of her, like a water balloon pricked by a pin. She still hadn't figured out how she was going to fit Tracey's party into her weekend. After her dressage lesson, she'd planned to spend most of Saturday helping around the farm. There was always a lot to do this time of year—splitting firewood, picking and canning squash and pumpkins and other vegetables from the garden, repairing and repainting fences, and raking the leaves that were already starting to gather in drifts as the nights grew cooler and the trees loosened their grip on their summer finery. Some of those were tasks that Haley was expected to help with as part of the family, while others would bring a few extra dollars for the clinic fund. Then on Saturday night, Haley had been thinking she could catch up on her reading for English class, study for next week's big math test, and take care of some of the other homework she'd been putting off. Now? She'd be lucky to get half of that done.

She glanced up as Tracey burst into the room. "Oh my gosh, I thought I was going to be late!" Tracey exclaimed breathlessly, dropping into her seat beside Emma. "Mom and I were making a shopping list for Saturday—she's hitting the craft store and the beverage place today—and I missed the bus, so she had to drive me."

"How's the party prep going?" Emma asked.

"Great." Tracey sat back in her seat, looking pleased with herself. "There's still a ton to do, though. I was thinking you guys should come over after school. We can figure out the final menu and pick out what music we want to play and stuff. And start figuring out decorations, too."

"Sure, that sounds fun," Emma said. "What kind of decorations are you doing?"

Tracey shrugged. "I told Mom to get a bunch of different stuff. I mean, it's not going to be like a little kid party, with streamers and balloons or whatever. But the place should look special, right?"

"Totally," Emma agreed.

Tracey finally seemed to notice that Haley hadn't said anything. "So you'll both come, right?" she demanded.

Haley gulped. "Uh, I can't. I didn't get a chance to ride this morning, so I have to do it later."

"You can skip one ride, can't you?" Tracey said. "I thought you gave Wings a day off sometimes anyway."

"I do, but he already had Monday off."

Tracey rolled her eyes. "So give him two days off this week. He won't shrivel up and die, will he?"

Haley shook her head. "Normally that would be okay, but we're on a pretty strict schedule right now because of the clinic. Wings is nice and fit, but I really want him in peak condition next Saturday, and if we don't get our trot sets done today, we might not have time to fit any in soon enough without skipping something else, and . . ."

She let her voice trail off, realizing the details didn't matter. Her friends were staring at her as if she'd suddenly sprouted an extra head.

"Okay, whatever," Tracey said. "I guess we could do it tomorrow instead. That won't leave us much time if we figure out we need anything else from the store, but—"

"Sorry," Haley broke in. "I'm babysitting right after

school tomorrow. I'll barely have enough time to get on Wings before dark as it is."

"Oh, come on." Tracey was starting to sound irritated. "Don't tell me you can't skip that ride either!"

"I can't." Haley picked at a splinter on her desk, her mind skittering back and forth over her packed schedule. "I've got my dressage lesson on Saturday, and I need to school him for it, but if I wait until Friday, that'll be dressage two days in a row, and that always gets him all wound up."

"Besides, Friday is the dance," Emma piped up. "You won't want to miss that, right?"

Haley hesitated. "Actually . . ."

Tracey let out a sound that was halfway between a snort and a yelp. "This is getting ridiculous," she exclaimed. "Look, Hales. As your friend, I'm telling you, you're getting out of control." She reached around Emma to poke Haley sharply in the shoulder. "So snap out of it! You're giving that horse of yours a day off today and coming to my house after school—no ifs, ands, or buts. Got it?"

Emma giggled, though her pale eyes were slightly

nervous. "Uh-oh," she said. "You'd better not argue with Tracey when she takes that tone!"

But Haley had known Tracey for a long time, and she wasn't intimidated by "that tone" at all. In fact, she tended to get extra stubborn whenever Tracey got like this—trying to bulldoze her way into getting what she wanted. Did she really think Haley was blowing her off for no good reason? Had she even *tried* to think about it from Haley's perspective? Leaning forward to see past Emma, Haley glared at Tracey.

"Maybe you didn't hear me the first time," she said evenly. "I can't come today. Or tomorrow, either. End of story."

"Fine." Tracey glared back, her lower lip pouting out like it always did when she didn't get her way. "Whatever. That just means more work for the two of us."

She turned away, pretending to be very busy searching for something in her backpack. Emma shot her a worried glance, then leaned toward Haley.

"Don't worry," she whispered. "She's just stressed over the party. She'll get over it—I'm sure we can get everything done without you today."

"Yeah." Haley sighed and sat back in her seat. She understood that Tracey was disappointed that they couldn't do this together like they normally would. She totally understood that.

So why couldn't Tracey at least try to understand Haley's point of view too?

• CHAPTER •
7

FRIDAY AFTERNOON JAKE CAME INTO THE barn while Haley was tightening Wings's girth. "Mom wants me to remind you that Mr. Broom is expecting you in like two hours," he said, leaning down to give Bandit a scratch as the dog bounded over to him.

"I know." Haley pulled the girth up one more notch, then let the saddle flap fall into place over it. Brushing off her hands, she glanced at her cousin. "Tell her I'll be back in plenty of time. I just want to get Wings over a few jumps today—we haven't been cross-country all week, and it'll settle him for our dressage lesson tomorrow."

"Whatever." Her cousin gave Bandit one last pat, then

headed for the exit. "Just don't get so excited jumping over logs and stuff that you forget the chicken poo extravaganza that's waiting for you."

Haley grimaced. She wasn't looking forward to cleaning out her uncle's friend's henhouse, but at least he was paying her well for the dirty job. And even though the neighbors had paid her more than she was expecting for babysitting their rambunctious toddler the day before, she wasn't taking anything for granted. Oh well—at least Mr. Broom had wanted her to wait until he got home from work before she started. That meant she and Wings got to go out and have some fun first.

"Ready, boy?" she asked the pony as Jake disappeared out the barn door. "I'll get your bridle."

Bandit trotted in circles around her as she walked to the tack room. He'd been underfoot since Haley had come outside after school, seeming extra restless and bored. She smiled at him as he followed her back out to the crossties.

"You look like you need something to do, buddy," she told the dog. "Want to come out with us today?"

Bandit cocked his head and gazed at her. Then he let

out an excited yip. Haley laughed. Sometimes she swore the dog was smart enough to understand English!

Anyway, it would be fun to have him along. She was planning to warm up with some brisk trots and canters on her way out to her cross-country field. She and Wings hadn't been out there since the previous Friday—she'd been focusing more on conditioning work, along with plenty of dressage and show jumping practice in the dirt pen behind the barn. A cross-country school would be just what they both needed right now to remind them why they were doing all that other stuff!

She held the main pasture's gate open so Bandit could follow her and Wings through, latching it behind them since the quarter horses were grazing out there. Then she swung into the saddle and set off. Wings was feeling good, almost immediately breaking into a trot without being asked. Haley let him go, smiling as Bandit dashed back and forth ahead of them, keeping busy by flushing birds and sniffing at every rock and desiccated cow patty they passed.

Haley slowed the pony to a walk when they reached

the tree line. It was a bright, clear day, and sunlight dappled the ground through the pines' lacy branches. Bandit barked at a squirrel scurrying up one of the trees, staying behind to sniff at it until Haley and Wings had almost reached the end of the patch of woods.

But a whistle brought the dog bounding after them again, and they were all together as they emerged through an open gate into the jumping pasture. Haley smiled as Wings lifted his head, immediately focusing on a roll-top jump lying just a few yards ahead. She was tempted to aim him at the jump right away but held back, doing a few circles and other figures at trot and canter to make sure he was warmed up and listening.

Finally, though, she couldn't resist any longer. "Okay, boy," she said. "Let's go!"

She aimed him first at a smallish log flanked by a pair of old barrels. Wings locked onto the obstacle right away, surging forward eagerly. Haley steadied him, making sure they'd meet the jump out of stride. They sailed over, and she was already turning him to the left as they landed.

"Tire jump next, big boy," she said aloud, thought she

doubted the pony could hear her over the wind rushing past as he cantered boldly on.

The jump over the homemade tire obstacle went just as well as the first. As Wings landed, Haley heard a bark from behind her. She glanced back just in time to see Bandit sailing over the tires just a few strides behind the pony!

Haley laughed out loud. "Go, Bandit!" she cried. "You're almost ready for your first beginner novice horse trials!"

The dog put on a burst of speed, catching up as Haley sat back and pulsed her reins to slow the pony's big stride. The next jump she wanted to do was the one known as a coffin. That was a tricky combination consisting of a sturdy wooden rail jump, then a downhill stride to a ditch, followed by an uphill stride to another rail. If they met the first jump too fast, it would mess up their distances for the rest.

"Easy, bub," she murmured, half-halting to shorten Wings's stride a little more.

The pony responded, his canter becoming bouncier and shorter without losing impulsion. Out of the corner of her eye, Haley could see that Bandit was still right beside them.

As Wings rounded over the first rail, Bandit leaped up, landing softly atop it before launching himself off the other side. Haley laughed again.

"Hey, wait for us!" she called as Wings landed, his ears already pricked toward the ditch.

Haley returned her attention to the pony, making sure their striding was perfect. But she was aware of Bandit matching them stride for stride and jump for jump. They all reached the far side of the combination together, and Bandit barked again as he and Wings both sped up joyfully. Wings snorted, tossed his head, and kicked up his heels, making Haley grin even as she kicked him forward.

Twenty minutes later, they'd jumped just about everything out there—some of the obstacles twice. As Wings landed after clearing a brush fence, Haley slowed him to a trot and then a walk. The pony was blowing a little, but Haley's careful conditioning routine had made him as fit as he'd ever been, and he still had plenty of energy left. After three or four flat-footed steps, he started jigging, trying to go faster again.

"No, that's enough for now." Haley loosened her reins and rubbed his withers, keeping him to a walk with her seat and voice. "We don't want to wear you out, or you won't have anything left for our dressage lesson in the morning."

She glanced down at Bandit, who'd stopped to scratch his ear. Haley couldn't wait to tell her Pony Post friends about the dog's cross-country schooling! She only wished they could have seen it for themselves.

That gave her an idea. Her cell phone was in her back pocket, as usual. Pulling it out, she quickly snapped a few photos of Bandit.

"Okay, Wingsie," she said. "Maybe we can do one more jump. . . ."

She trotted him toward a stack of logs. The pony tried to break into a canter, but she kept him at a trot.

Just as she'd expected, Bandit raced ahead of them, barking loudly. Holding the reins in one hand, Haley snapped another photo just as the dog sailed over the log jump. She laughed as Bandit landed—and immediately spun around, jumping the logs again coming toward her! Luckily, Haley's phone was still in position, and she got off another couple of shots before Wings reached his takeoff spot.

On the far side of the jump, Haley stopped the pony and scrolled through the pictures. She couldn't see the tiny monitor very well in the bright sunshine, but she was pretty sure she'd captured some good shots.

"Next time I'll have to try taking some video," she told Wings and Bandit with a laugh. "Too bad Nina isn't closer—she's such a good photographer, I bet she could film us. Or maybe I could talk someone else into coming out sometime with a camera."

Her smile wavered slightly as her mind flashed from her Pony Post friends to her local ones. Now that they were all about boys and parties, would Tracey or Emma still be interested in watching her ride?

But no—she wasn't going to think about that right then and spoil her happy mood. Gathering up the reins, she nudged Wings into a trot.

"Okay, you win," she said. "I suppose we still have time for a few more jumps before we have to head back."

◆ ◆ ◆

"Urgh," Haley grunted as her phone buzzed in her pocket. She set aside the wide, square-headed shovel she'd been using to chip away at the dried chicken manure on the henhouse floor. Mr. Broom had gone off to dump the tractor bucket, which he and Haley had filled with yet another load of soiled bedding. Outside in the attached pen, Haley could hear the chickens clucking and burbling irritably, clearly wondering why the door into their house was shut. It was after six thirty already, and they would be wanting to roost soon.

Peeling off one glove, she carefully fished the phone out and hit the button to answer it. She stepped outside, taking in a breath of welcome fresh air.

"Hello?" she said.

"Are you sure you're not coming? Ems and I are at her house getting dressed. We're leaving in like ten minutes."

Haley sighed. She didn't need to check the readout to know who it was. Tracey sounded hopeful, as if she might actually be expecting Haley to change her mind and come to the dance.

She wouldn't think that if she could see me—or smell me—right now, Haley thought, glancing down at herself. Her jeans, shirt, and skin were spattered with ick, and a thin layer of the dust that always seemed to hang around chickens covered her from head to boot.

"Sorry, still can't," she told Tracey. "You guys have fun, though. I want to hear everything tomorrow."

"For sure." Tracey hesitated. "So you're still coming to my party, though, right?"

"Of course," Haley answered, not allowing any impatience to creep into her voice.

"Cool. So you're really not coming tonight?" Tracey sounded as if she still couldn't quite believe it.

"Really." Haley could hear the sound of the tractor heading back her way. Her stomach rumbled, complaining about her delayed dinner. "Look, I have to go. Have a great time, okay?"

Haley didn't get home from Mr. Broom's place until almost eight. All she wanted to do was gobble down about three pounds of food, then fall into bed, in that order. Okay, maybe she'd slip a shower in there some-where—she hadn't felt so filthy since the last time she'd helped move the manure pile.

"I'm home!" she called to her uncle, who was washing dishes and singing along with the radio. Aunt Veronica was nowhere in sight, which meant she was probably in her office getting some work done. The sound of the TV drifted up from the basement, and Haley hoped that meant both boys were down there. The last thing she was in the mood for was teasing from them about her current state of stinkiness.

She said hi to Uncle Mike and then dragged herself up the steps, grabbing a fresh bath towel from the linen closet as she headed down the hall to her room. Her nightgown was slung over the back of her desk chair where she'd dropped it that morning. As she grabbed it, she noticed her laptop sitting on the desk and flipped it open.

I'd better check the Pony Post now, she told herself. *I'll be too tired later, and who knows if I'll have even an extra two seconds tomorrow.*

For a moment, she felt even more exhausted as she

thought about everything she had to fit in the next day. But she banished the thought, her fingers flying over the keys as she logged on to the Pony Post.

As usual, there were plenty of new messages. Haley skimmed most of them, but her gaze caught on one from Nina.

[NINA] Big news, pony peeps! Breezy and I had a lesson today, and guess what? I found out there's going to be a horse show at my barn next month!

[MADDIE] Cool! Are u going to enter?

[BROOKE] Of course she is! Wait, N, will this be yr 1st show?

[MADDIE] I think it is! Nina? Paging Nina! Don't leave us hanging!

[NINA] lol, sorry I was offline for a few hours. A girl has to eat, u know! Anyway, ya, this will be my first show. Well, my first horse show, anyway.

I've been in lots of other kinds of shows!

[MADDIE] lol, we don't want to hear about all

yr dance recitals or whatev right now, OK?

Spill! What kind of show is it going to be?

Haley skimmed another few entries from Nina, detailing what she knew about the coming show. She was excited for her friend—Nina had owned her Chincoteague pony, a stout bay pinto gelding named Bay Breeze, for less than two years now. She hadn't been riding for as long as Haley or Brooke, who had both learned to ride almost before they could walk. But she was learning fast, and Haley was sure she couldn't wait to show off what a good team she and her pony had become.

Kind of like me and Wings, she thought as she scrolled down to the next post. *I just hope Zina Charles sees that next weekend!*

She shivered, thinking of the clinic, just one week

away now! Then she returned her attention to the computer screen. She spotted her name in Maddie's next post.

[MADDIE] U can get some show pointers from Haley. She's prolly been in more shows than the rest of us put together!

[BROOKE] That's for sure! I've only been in two—a student show where I used to take lessons, and then the one at the end of camp this summer.

[MADDIE] I did a student show with Cloudy last spring too. Of course, Haley prolly thinks we're all big wimps since the jumps in our shows fall down if we hit them, unlike those crazy XC things she and Wings jump!

[NINA] lol, ya. Well, that's why she's getting ready to ride in a clinic with a future Olympic champion, and I'm just hoping

I can hold on over a few crossrails w/o

embarrassing myself or my pony! LOL!

[BROOKE] LOL! Don't worry, u can do it!

Haley smiled. That was the latest post, sent just an hour or so earlier. Opening a new text box, she started typing.

[HALEY] Nina, that's awesome news! I know

u will do great at yr show. Can't wait to see

pics of u and Breezy showing yr stuff!

She sent the message. It appeared on the screen, blinking at the bottom of her friends' long list of posts. Haley reached for the touch screen to sign off, but instead moved her hand back to the keyboard and opened another text box.

[HALEY] btw, sorry I haven't been posting

more. It's crazy how busy things are right now.

I don't know how ZC and other pro riders do

it!!! I'll prob be even busier for the next wk, but

I promise to make up for it after the clinic!

This time she did sign off as soon as the message showed up. Her friends were probably all in bed by now, so she shouldn't expect a response until tomorrow.

Besides, Haley already knew what they'd say. She knew they'd understand why she'd been a little out of touch—and they wouldn't mind. After all, they all took turns posting more or less often on the Pony Post. When Maddie had been so busy trying to buy Cloudy, she hadn't posted nearly as much as usual. And of course, Brooke hadn't been able to log on very often when she and her pony, Foxy, were at that sleepaway riding camp over the summer. Nina had a fancy smartphone that let her check in easily anywhere, but even she sometimes got busy with school and art lessons and all the other stuff she did in her exciting big-city life.

But no matter how busy any of them got, they all kept coming back to the Pony Post. Because even though they lived far apart and were very different in some ways, their love for their ponies was one thing they'd always have in common.

After a shower and a quick dinner, Haley could barely keep her eyes open. She set her alarm, grimacing as she counted out the hours—not nearly enough—until she had to get up for her dressage lesson. She'd only managed to give her tack a quick once-over after that day's ride, but she figured Jan would understand.

She climbed into bed, her tired brain buzzing with everything she had to do tomorrow. If only she didn't have to fit that stupid party in with everything else! For a second she thought about telling Tracey she couldn't make it after all.

But no. For some mysterious reason, that party seemed to be just as important to Tracey as the clinic was to Haley. All Haley had to do was get through it—and everything else on her overcrowded schedule—for a little while longer. Because exactly one week from tomorrow, the clinic would be here, and all the hard work and lost sleep would be worth it.

◆ CHAPTER ◆
8

"GOOD BOY!" HALEY SAID AS WINGS LENGTH-
ened his trot stride along the fence. "Good, good boy!"

"Excellent!" her instructor called from the center of
the paddock Haley used as a riding ring. "You're looking
good today—both of you."

"Thanks!" Haley brought Wings back to a walk and
gave him a pat, feeling pleased. Jan Whipple was only
in her midthirties, but she definitely took after the old-
school horsemen who'd taught her when she was Haley's
age. That meant she wasn't the type of instructor to
give compliments unless she meant them. The first time
Haley had attempted the lengthening, all Jan had said

was, "Hmm. Again." But this time, a wide grin split her tanned, freckled face beneath its battered old Wisconsin Dairy Association ball cap.

"Okay," Jan called out. "Now pick up left lead canter at A." She winked. "Well, where A should be, anyway."

Haley had moved all the jump rails and standards out of the paddock a couple of days earlier after their last show jumping school, but she hadn't had time to lay out a real dressage ring, with letters marking the spots where transitions were supposed to happen. But that didn't really matter. They weren't practicing tests today, just schooling various movements.

And so far, Wings was doing great! When he'd first come to live with Haley, learning to jump had come easily to him. But he hadn't had much patience for the slow, intricate dressage work she'd started asking him to learn as well. In his old life with the neighbor's daughter, he hadn't been asked to do much other than run and circle around the barrels—turn and burn, as some barrel racers called it—with a little easy trail riding in between competitions.

But dressage was different. Riding a successful test

involved performing specific gaits, figures, and transitions as accurately as possible, and precision hadn't exactly been Wings's forte at the beginning. Or Haley's, either, for that matter. She loved running and jumping—that was why she'd been attracted to eventing in the first place. At first she'd considered dressage as just something to get through on the way to the fun stuff.

Then she and Wings had entered their first competition. It hadn't been anything big or fancy or recognized— just a tiny, informal starter horse trials at a lesson stable over in the next county. Wings had been a superstar at the jumping parts. He'd gone double clear in cross-country and stadium, barely seeming to notice the tiny elementary-level obstacles.

But the dressage test had been another matter. It was just a walk-trot test, and aside from memorizing it, Haley had barely bothered to prepare for it at all outside of her occasional lessons with Jan. And it had shown—they'd blown a couple of transitions, with Wings jumping into a canter once when he was supposed to be trotting. He'd also jigged through the halt, and their circles were shaped more like melting snowballs. They'd ended up with a pretty terrible score, which had dropped them out of the ribbons completely.

After that, Haley had taken dressage a lot more seriously. She'd even started to enjoy it most of the time. It helped that Jan was so enthusiastic about it, constantly pointing out all the ways that getting better at dressage would also improve their jumping. For instance, she'd first started teaching them lengthenings by asking Haley to trot or canter Wings between two poles or small jumps in different numbers of strides—doing the same distance once in five strides, then in six, then in four. Both Haley and Wings had found that exercise a lot of fun, and Haley had soon discovered that being able to adjust her pony's stride could come in handy out on cross-country as well.

They'd come a long way since then. Now their circles were mostly round and their transitions usually came at the right place. But there was always something new to work on!

The rest of that morning's lesson flew by. Haley was surprised when she checked her watch at the end and realized they'd gone fifteen minutes over the allotted time.

"Thanks so much for coming all the way over here to teach us today," she said as she stopped Wings beside Jan.

"You're welcome." Jan rubbed Wings's nose as he nudged at her, looking for treats. "I didn't mind a bit. It's not every day that a student of mine is getting ready to ride with Zina Charles."

Haley smiled. "I know, right? I can hardly believe it's really going to happen."

At least it will if I get everything done and earn enough money, she added silently, though she didn't say it to Jan.

"Well, I think you two are ready. I can tell you've been working hard," Jan said. "You and Wings have made a lot of progress since our last lesson."

"Thanks." Haley beamed and leaned forward to rub the pony's withers. "He's a superstar!"

"That he is." Jan dug a slightly dusty carrot-flavored horse treat out of her pocket and fed it to Wings. "I'll expect a full report after the clinic, okay?"

"Promise." Haley slid down from the saddle and ran up her stirrups. She'd pretty much forgotten about the rest of the world while she was riding, as usual. But now she was back to thinking about everything she still had to do before the clinic. There was no time to dawdle, especially today.

"Stay, Bandit." Haley closed the picket gate in the dog's face.

He whined at her from the barnyard, wagging his tail hopefully. But Haley knew better than to let him into the garden. The last time he'd sneaked in there, he'd dug up half of Aunt Veronica's prized irises and eaten all the blooms off her roses.

Haley reached over the gate to give Bandit one last ear scratch. Then she headed into the house. It was after four thirty already, and she would have to hurry if she was going to have time to take a shower, change clothes, and grab something to eat before Emma's mother came by to pick her up for Tracey's party.

Uncle Mike was still out in the barn changing the oil in the tractor, but Aunt Veronica was in the kitchen getting dinner started. "Tracey came by an hour or so ago," she told Haley. "Left you something. It's in your room."

"Okay, thanks." When she got upstairs, Haley found a garment bag lying on her bed. Unzipping it, she pulled out a flouncy floral skirt and a pale green blouse. A note was pinned to the front of the blouse, written in Tracey's big, loopy handwriting.

Surprise! I know u r busy, so I thought u could wear this. It will look cute on u! See u at the party!

After that came several hearts and flowers and smiley faces, followed by Tracey's signature. Haley glanced at the clothes, feeling both touched and annoyed. It had been nice of Tracey to take the time to figure out something for her to wear and drop it off, especially since she had to be pretty busy herself today. But couldn't she see that this outfit wasn't exactly Haley's style?

She dropped the garment bag on her bed and wandered to her closet. Swinging open the door, she stared blankly at the clothes inside.

Then she sighed and returned to the bed. She didn't

have the energy to come up with something else to wear. Tracey's outfit would have to do.

Half an hour later, Haley was showered and dressed. She headed downstairs, following the scent of roast beef.

When she entered the kitchen, everyone else was already at the table. "Wow!" Aunt Veronica said with a smile. "You look beautiful, Haley!"

Jake glanced up from shoveling mashed sweet potatoes into his mouth. "That's not Haley," he said through a mouthful of half-chewed food. "That's a girl."

"Yeah, where'd that girl come from?" Danny smirked. "We don't allow those around here."

Aunt Veronica shot them a sour look. "Enough, boys," she said.

"Sit down, Haley," Uncle Mike said. "Have some grub before you go." He winked at her. "Shrimp cocktails and dainty tea sandwiches won't fill you up after the long day you just put in."

Haley giggled as she slid into her seat. "I don't think Tracey's serving shrimp cocktails and tea sandwiches," she said. "But thanks, I am pretty hungry."

She filled her plate with food. Danny watched her, his fork suspended above his plate.

"Careful, Haley," he said. "If you eat too much, you might bust out of your froufrou flowery outfit."

"Daniel," his mother said warningly.

Haley ignored the boys as she ate. She'd barely taken the time to wolf down a sandwich at lunchtime, and it really had been a long day. After her dressage lesson, she'd mucked out all four stalls and rebedded them, followed by various other farm chores. Then her uncle had asked her to help him stack firewood and sweep out the machine shed, and Aunt Veronica had needed help carrying things down to the root cellar. After that Haley had dashed over to the Tompkins' to take care of their plants and cat, then rushed back to start the afternoon chores. It made her tired just thinking back on it all.

She'd just finished her third helping of sweet potatoes when a car horn sounded outside. "Oops, that must be Ems." Haley quickly wiped her mouth with her napkin, then jumped to her feet and picked up her plate.

"Leave that, Haley." Her aunt pulled the plate out of her hands and set it down. "The boys will clear."

"What?" Danny exclaimed, sounding annoyed.

Aunt Veronica ignored him, standing up and adjusting Haley's ponytail. "You really do look pretty, sweetie," she said. "Have a nice time tonight, okay?"

"I'll try." With some effort, Haley managed not to grimace. Her aunt was right—she was stuck going to this party, like it or not. She might as well at least try to have a good time.

An hour and a half later, Haley stifled a yawn as she checked her watch for about the fifteenth time. It felt as if she'd been at Tracey's party forever. Despite her best efforts, she couldn't seem to stop thinking about all the much more important stuff she could be doing right now. She'd wiped down her dressage saddle before her lesson that morning, but there had been no time to give it a proper cleaning and oiling. And of course she hadn't touched her jumping saddle at all. She hadn't managed to get Wings's mane pulled yet either, or polished her tall boots, or dug through her tack trunk for her good crop and helmet cover. . . .

"Haley!" Emma danced over, holding a plastic cup of punch. "Isn't this a blast?"

Emma's face was flushed, and her glasses kept getting steamed up. But she seemed to be having fun. Haley wasn't sure why. The party seemed to consist of people standing around shouting at each other over the too-loud dance music. Only a handful of people were actually dancing. Ashley and Phil, their grade's only official couple, were swaying together in one corner, arms wrapped around each other. Emma had been fast dancing with Tracey and a few other girls for a while, though most of the group had drifted off to pick at the snacks laid out on the coffee table, which had been pushed up against the living room wall along with most of the other furniture. It was drizzling outside, which meant everyone was crammed indoors instead of the party spilling out onto the deck as Tracey had planned, and the place felt stuffy and too warm.

"Where's Tracey?" Haley asked Emma.

"What?" Emma scrunched up her face and leaned closer. "I can't hear you!"

"I said, where's Tracey?" Haley shouted into her ear.

Emma shrugged and glanced around. "I don't know—wait, there she is!"

Now Haley saw her too. Tracey was winding her way through the crowd, pulling Owen along by one wrist.

"There you are!" Tracey exclaimed when she reached Haley and Emma. "I've been looking everywhere for you, Hales!"

Haley doubted that. For one thing, she'd seen Tracey giggling and leaning against Nick Jankowski just a short while earlier. For another, Haley herself had been standing right there in the arched doorway leading to the kitchen hallway for at least the past fifteen minutes.

But she just smiled weakly. "Here I am."

Tracey dragged Owen forward. "So I was just telling Owen about your clinic thingy," she said. "Ooh! I love this song!"

The music had just changed to an up-tempo number with a pounding beat, though Haley noticed that Ashley and Phil were still swaying to their own tune. Tracey started dancing in place as she poked Owen on the arm.

"So anyway," she said loudly, "I figured he'd be totally impressed, since you guys both spend all your time riding horses and stuff."

"Well, sort of." Owen smirked. "*I* ride horses. Haley prances around on a runt of a pony."

Haley rolled her eyes. "My runt of a pony could outrun and outjump your lazy horse any day of the week," she said.

It was a familiar exchange. But tonight, Haley's heart wasn't really in it. Why was she here? She had too much on her plate right now to spend hours standing around doing nothing.

"Yo, Vance!" Owen whistled as one of his friends wandered past. "Get over here. Did you hear Haley's doing a clinic with some fancy member of the tight pants club?"

"Huh?" Vance was a large, slow-moving boy who always looked sleepy. Despite that, he was one of the best under-fourteen ropers in the county. "What're you talking about?"

"Haley's taking a lesson with an Olympic rider next week!" Tracey told him, still swaying to the music.

"She hasn't been to the Olympics yet," Haley corrected. "Probably someday, though."

Vance blinked. "The Olympics? So you're doing reining now?"

"Reining? No way." Owen grinned. "That'd be way too cool for Haley. She's into the goofy English stuff, remember?"

"Oh, right." A slow grin spread across Vance's face. "Jumping over flowers and stuff, right?"

Tracey giggled. "Oh, you guys!" she exclaimed, giving Vance a playful shove.

Haley stared at her. Where had this weird, giggly, boy-crazy girl come from? And what had she done with her best friend?

"Actually, that reminds me," Haley said loudly. "I have to get up early to get a ride in before church. So I should probably go."

"What? No!" Tracey's eyes widened in alarm. "You can't go now—the party's barely getting started!"

"Yeah," Emma put in. "We haven't even had a chance to tell you about the dance yet either! Besides, you can't leave—you rode here with me, remember? And Mom's not coming to pick us up until ten."

Haley was already reaching for her cell phone. "I'm sure Uncle Mike will come get me."

Tracey frowned. "Whatever."

"Yeah, whatever," Owen put in with a smirk. "Hope I didn't scare you off. If you were a real Western rider, you could take a little joke."

"If you were any kind of real rider at all, you wouldn't care what kind of saddle I rode in," Haley shot back. "But that's not why I'm leaving, so don't flatter yourself."

Vance chuckled and punched Haley on the arm. "Good one, Haley."

Haley smiled weakly, trying not to notice the confused look on Emma's face or the stormy one on Tracey's. Lifting a hand to wave good-bye, she hurried out into the relative quiet of the kitchen to call home.

◆ ◆ ◆

"Still awake, buddy?" Haley said as Bandit came rushing forward to greet her.

It was well after nine o'clock, and the barn was quiet. Uncle Mike had left the horses out in the pasture for the night, since the weather was still mild and the light rain had already stopped. It wouldn't be long until the cooler weather stopped the grass from growing, and he wanted to save the hay stores he'd laid in as long as possible. Haley knew the horses liked being out, but she wished Wings was in his stall so she could give him a hug and let him help her remember why she was still awake instead of snuggled into her comfortable bed.

For a moment she considered walking out to the pasture and whistling him over. But then a giant yawn overtook her, and she decided that would be too much effort. In fact, she almost turned around and headed back into the house. But if she put off her tack cleaning, she'd just have to fit it in later. Better to get it out of the way now.

Bandit followed as Haley headed into the tack room. One of the cats was curled up on the stack of Western saddle blankets, and Haley gave her a quick pat. Then she reached for her tack-cleaning bucket, which was still sitting by the doorway where she'd left it that morning. She pulled down her jumping saddle and set it on the handmade wooden rack in the middle of the room. Grabbing the antique milking stool passed down from the days when the farm was a dairy, she sat down and set to work.

✦ CHAPTER ✦
9

"ALMOST FINISHED WITH THOSE BOOTS?" Uncle Mike stuck his head into Haley's bedroom on Sunday night. "It's getting late, and tomorrow's a school day."

"I'm done." Haley gave her tall riding boots one last wipe with a cloth, then sat back, gazing at them in satisfaction. They were old and well-worn hand-me-downs from one of Jan's other students who'd outgrown them, but they were good quality. The cleaning and polish Haley had just done made the leather gleam as if the boots were brand-new.

That's another thing I can check off my to-do list, Haley thought as she set the boots aside and wiped her hands on the rag. It had been another long, tiring day, but she'd accomplished a lot and was feeling pretty good. At church that morning, her aunt had been chatting with a neighbor who'd mentioned she was looking to hire someone to come and transplant some perennials before the cold weather set in. Haley had volunteered, and while the job had taken longer than expected, the woman had also given her ten dollars more than she'd promised. Sure, that meant Haley had been behind on everything else she had to do, but it was worth it.

She'd been so busy that she hadn't had much time to worry about whether Tracey was going to be mad at her for leaving the party early. Neither she nor Emma had called or texted all day, which told Haley that the answer was probably yes.

She grabbed her nightgown off her chair, revealing her school backpack below. With a gulp, she realized she hadn't done any homework all weekend aside from dashing off the social studies worksheet in the car on the way home on Friday. But that was okay, she told herself as she rifled through the bag. She could do the reading for

English class in the car tomorrow morning, and . . .

"Oh no!" she said aloud. "The math test!"

Panic washed over her. How could she have forgotten about the big test tomorrow? While Aunt Veronica and Uncle Mike were pretty easygoing about most things, they took school seriously. Once when Jake had forgotten to turn in a school project, they'd grounded him for an entire month and made him quit the baseball team. If they found out Haley had blown an important test, they might not let her go to the clinic next weekend! They might not even let her ride until she brought her grade up!

She couldn't take that chance. Quickly pulling on her nightgown, she grabbed her math textbook and crawled into bed, hiding the book under the covers. A moment later Aunt Veronica knocked and stuck her head in.

"Lights out, sweetie," she said, flicking the switch by the door. "See you in the morning."

"Night," Haley said.

She waited until the hall light went off, then a few minutes more to make sure the house was quiet. Then she turned on the lamp on her bedside table and pulled out her math book. Flipping to the chapter on percentages, she did her best to focus on the words and numbers on the page.

But math wasn't Haley's best subject even when she wasn't completely exhausted. And tonight her tired brain just couldn't seem to take in what it was reading. Within minutes she was completely confused, her mind swirling with ratios and numeric values and all sorts of other terms she didn't really understand. How was she ever going to learn this stuff before tomorrow?

I can't do it, she thought hopelessly. *I'm going to flunk that test, and then the clinic is toast. I'll miss my chance to ride with Zina, and Wings will miss his chance to really show off what he can do, and all our hard work over the past few weeks will have been for nothing, and we'll never make it past beginner novice....*

Haley wasn't much of a crier, but tears came to her eyes now. It just wasn't fair! She was so close to making her dreams come true. She couldn't let some stupid math test stop her!

She glanced at the door. Aunt Veronica was a whiz at math. So was Jake, for that matter. But they were both in bed. How mad would they be if she woke them up?

Pretty mad, she admitted with a sigh.

Seeing her laptop sitting on the desk, she wondered if she could find some kind of free math help site online. Then she had a better idea.

Hopping out of bed, she grabbed the laptop and logged on to the Pony Post. Brooke and Maddie were both great at math too. Maybe one of them could help her! While the site was loading, she checked the time. It was almost eleven thirty on the East Coast, which meant Brooke was surely in bed. But it was only eight thirty in California. . . .

She crossed her fingers as the site appeared and felt a rush of hope as she saw that the most recent entry was from Maddie. Before she could check the time stamp on the post, a photo suddenly popped into view. It showed a cute palomino pinto pony wearing a sun visor on her head and a Hawaiian-style lei around her neck. A moment later a text entry appeared below it.

[MADDIE] What do u all think? This is the last pic of possible Halloween costumes for Cloudy.

Cute, right? I know Halloween is still weeks

away, but I want to be ready, lol! Anyway, it's

getting late, so I'll chat w/u all tomorrow!

"Wait!" Haley blurted aloud.

Her fingers flew over the keys. Seconds later she jabbed
at the enter key, and her post appeared.

[HALEY] Mads, wait! Don't sign off yet!

She held her breath, watching the screen. Was she too
late?

Then another post popped up.

[MADDIE] I'm still here! What's up?
Isn't it past bedtime where u are?

Haley let out the breath she was holding and smiled.
Then she started typing again.

[HALEY] Yes, it is. That's why I need ur help!

She kept typing, explaining the issue. Maddie caught on quickly, asking Haley for the name of her textbook so she could look it up on the Internet. It turned out she'd studied percentages at the end of the previous school year, and she assured Haley that she'd be able to learn it too.

[MADDIE] U are sooo organized and logical about stuff, this should be cake for u. Just pretend u need to figure out something to do w/Wings. Like, what percentage of his feed is beet pulp vs. sweet feed or whatev? Or: what percentage of your last ride did u spend on jumping vs. flatwork?

[HALEY] That's easy—but I don't get graded on what I feed my pony or how much I jump him! LOL!

[MADDIE] lol, I know. But just go with it, okay? Here's how u turn that kind of percentage question into the same kind of equation you'll prolly see on yr test. . . .

Haley rubbed her eyes as she read on, nodding slowly. Somehow, the way Maddie explained the concepts made much more sense than the way the textbook did. Or grouchy, impatient old Mr. Washington, for that matter.

Half an hour later, she was pretty sure she was starting to get it. Maddie had talked her through some of the problems in the chapter, and the concepts were almost starting to make sense.

[MADDIE] Oops, my mom just told
me it's time to turn off the computer.
Should I ask her if I can stay on a
little longer, or are u OK now?

[HALEY] I think I'll be OK. Thanks, Maddie.
U saved my life—and my clinic!

[MADDIE] Anytime. That's what friends r for!

◆ ◆ ◆

"Haley? Haley! Wake up."

Haley swam out of a deep, dark sleep. Something was buzzing around her head. A giant bee? No, wait, it was her alarm, the sound attacking her like a physical threat. She reached out from under the covers and swatted at it.

"Ow," she mumbled as she hit the corner of her bedside table instead.

A second later the alarm stopped.

"Haley."

Haley cracked open one eye and saw Aunt Veronica gazing down at her. "Um, hmm . . . ," Haley mumbled.

Her aunt crossed her arms. "Your alarm has been going off for ten minutes," she said. "Didn't you hear it?"

Haley sat up and rubbed her eyes. "It was? Sorry." Noticing her English book lying on the floor beside her bed, she hoped her aunt didn't see it. After signing off with Maddie, Haley had studied her math for another half hour or so, then decided to get a head start on the reading for tomorrow. She must have dozed off in the middle of it.

Her aunt looked concerned. "You look tired," she said.

"You're running yourself ragged doing all this extra work lately. I'll tell the boys they can do their own morning chores today."

"No!" Suddenly Haley felt much more awake. "It's okay, I'm fine. I'll do them." She was feeling pretty good about her finances after earning that extra money the day before, but she didn't want to take any chances. If she didn't do the boys' chores, she wouldn't get paid. It would be heartbreaking if that turned out to be the difference between having enough to cover the clinic and having to stay home.

She climbed out of bed, stifling her yawn until her aunt had bustled out of the room. Pulling on her robe, she stuffed her English and math books into her backpack. She might be tired, but at least she was feeling a little more confident about that test. Maddie had really helped her understand the math chapter last night, and Haley figured she could finish the rest of the English reading in the car and in homeroom, and then do some last-minute cramming for the math test at lunch.

That shouldn't be a problem, she thought. *Tracey and Emma probably still won't be talking to me anyhow.*

A few minutes later Haley was in the barn. The horses had spent the night outside again, and for a second the thought of walking out there to get Wings made her feel so tired she nearly collapsed where she stood.

Then she remembered: It was Monday. The pony's day off from riding.

"Whew," she murmured, leaning against a support beam for a moment.

The feeling of a cold nose against her hand snapped her out of it. Glancing down, she saw Bandit nudging at her.

"Ready for your breakfast?" she asked the dog with a yawn. "I guess I'll feed you guys first, then do the other chores."

Soon the dogs and cats were fed. Haley let the chickens out, scattering a few handfuls of cracked corn for them to peck at. Then she stood there for a moment, trying to remember what else she had to do. With a groan, she recalled that the big stock tank had been getting low last night and would need to be topped off this morning. Hurrying out to the pasture, she slipped between the fence boards and dropped the hose into the tank. The hydrant was always sticky, but today it seemed extra hard to pry up the handle. Letting out a grunt, she finally got the water turned on.

She returned to the barn while the tank filled. At least the stalls weren't very dirty, since they hadn't been occupied the night before. But nobody had mucked them out after the horses had come in for dinner the evening before, and there were a few piles of manure already attracting flies. For a moment Haley was tempted to leave cleaning them until after school.

Then she remembered that Mrs. Vandenberg had called yesterday after dinner asking if Haley could watch the triplets this afternoon. That meant she would have to get the stalls done now.

With a wide yawn, she went to fetch the wheelbarrow. It felt heavy as she pushed it into the doorway of Chico's stall. She yawned again as she scooped up a manure pile with the fork. She'd just tossed the manure into the barrow when Bandit trotted into the stall and pressed himself up against her leg.

"Out," Haley ordered, giving him a shove with her foot. "No time to play today."

Bandit whined, his fringed tail wagging slowly as he gazed at her. She shook her head.

"I'm serious. Go!" She made her voice stern and pointed to the aisle.

With one last whine, Bandit slunk back out. But he didn't go far—Haley had to stop the wheelbarrow to avoid running it into him when she moved on to the next stall.

"Go!" she exclaimed. "Get out of here, Bandit!"

The dog finally wandered off and Haley sighed, feeling slightly guilty for losing her temper with the dog. Oh well—too late now. She'd make it up to him after the clinic, maybe take him out trail riding in the woods or something.

It didn't take long to pick out all the stalls. Still, when she checked her watch she saw that she was running late. She'd need to hurry if she wanted to have time for even a quick breakfast.

Leaving the wheelbarrow where it stood, she rushed around getting everything else done. She was so tired that she almost dropped the basket while she was collecting the eggs, and she tripped over the same cat twice while she was watering the window boxes on the henhouse.

But finally, she was pretty sure everything was done except dumping the wheelbarrow. She grabbed the handles and rushed it across the barnyard. As she reached the gate, she suddenly thought about something. Had she turned off the water to the stock tank, or was it still running?

She bit her lip, willing her tired brain to remember as she swung open the gate and shoved the barrow through. She pushed the wheelbarrow toward the manure heap slowly, still trying to picture whether she'd shut off the hydrant and coiled up the hose, or . . .

Screee . . . CRASH!

A sudden squeal of car brakes from the road startled Haley out of her sleepy thoughts. With a gasp, she whirled around—and saw a limp, furry shape lying in the road just a few yards away.

"Oh no—Bandit!" she blurted out, glancing from the gate—standing wide open where she'd forgotten to close it—back to her favorite dog's still body.

◆ CHAPTER ◆
10

"PLEASE, PLEASE, PLEASE BE OKAY, BANDIT." Haley's voice was shaky as she stroked the dog's blood-matted fur. Bandit was stretched across the backseat of her aunt's car, his head in Haley's lap. He was trembling, and his eyes were cloudy with pain. Even so, his tail thumped against the vinyl seat every time Haley said his name.

Uncle Mike glanced at the pair in the rearview mirror. "Hang in there, sport," he said, his voice gruff with sympathy. "We'll be at Doc Hagen's place in five minutes. Your aunt's calling ahead, so he'll be expecting us."

Haley just nodded, too choked up to speak. How could she have been so stupid, so careless? She knew Bandit was always trying to follow her everywhere she went, and she knew how dangerous the highway could be, especially during the morning rush. How could she have forgotten to shut the gate behind her? Her gaze wandered to Bandit's left hind leg, which seemed to be lying at an unnatural angle.

Her eyes filled with tears as she looked at the dog. At least her aunt and uncle had agreed to let her be late to school to go to the vet. She couldn't have stood not knowing what was going on.

The local small animal vet's clinic was located in his grand old Victorian house on the edge of town. The parking area was empty when they pulled in.

"Hang on," Uncle Mike said as he cut the engine. "I'll help you carry him in."

The clinic door swung open as Haley and her uncle carefully carried the dog between them on the old bath towel they were using as a makeshift stretcher. Dr. Hagen was in his late fifties, with kind blue eyes and a gentle way with animals.

"Easy, there," he said. "Poor old Bandit. Bring him right in. . . ."

Ten minutes later Haley held her breath as the vet finished his examination and straightened up. "Well?" Uncle Mike said quietly.

Dr. Hagen's expression was somber as he gave Bandit a gentle pat on his head. "You won't be surprised to hear the leg is fractured," he said. "That alone might not be so bad, but I'm pretty sure the hip is cracked too. That'll require immediate surgery if we want to save him."

"Of course we want to save him!" Haley blurted out. She looked from the vet to her uncle. "Of course we do! Right?"

Uncle Mike rubbed his chin, not quite meeting her eye. "What're we talking, doc?"

"Unfortunately, it won't be cheap," the veterinarian said.

"Nothing ever is." Uncle Mike smiled, but it looked strained. "Lay it on me."

Haley gasped aloud as the vet named a number. Uncle Mike winced. "That's a lot of money, doc," he said quietly.

"But we can do it," Haley said urgently, staring from one man to the other. "Right? We have to!"

Uncle Mike hesitated. He closed his eyes for a moment, then stepped over and squeezed Haley's shoulder. "I'm sorry, Haley," he said, his voice hoarse and low. "I wish we could. But that kind of money just isn't in the family budget right now. Might be better to let him go."

"What? You mean put him to sleep? No!" Haley was barely aware that she was crying. She stepped over and ran her hands over Bandit's soft fur. The vet had sedated him, but his tail twitched at her touch.

"I'm very sorry," Dr. Hagen said. "I'll give you a moment."

He stepped out of the exam room. Uncle Mike came over and stroked Bandit's head, his kind hazel eyes stricken.

"You know we'd do it if we could, Haley," he said. "Bandit's a good dog. But with the tractor payments, and—"

"I'll pay for it," Haley blurted out before she even knew what she was going to say.

Her uncle blinked, looking startled. "What's that now?"

Haley took a deep breath and squared her shoulders. "I said, I'll pay for the surgery," she said. "I have just about enough saved up."

"Oh." Uncle Mike shook his head. "But that money's for your riding clinic. This means—"

"I know," Haley said before he could continue. She couldn't stand to hear him say it out loud. "I know. It's okay. There will be other clinics. But there's only one Bandit." Her fingers ran lightly up the dog's familiar snout and over his sleek head. It was strange to see him lying so still, when normally he never stopped moving.

Her uncle took a deep breath. "Let me call your aunt and get her input," he said.

He stepped out into the waiting room with his cell phone, leaving Haley alone with Bandit. She leaned over the dog, willing him to hang on just a little longer.

"I'm so sorry, buddy," she whispered, burying her fingers in his fur. "It's all my fault you're hurt. But I'm going to make it better—promise."

She stared at him, picturing him jumping those cross-country obstacles right alongside Wings the other day. Thinking about that ride, about how much fun she'd had doing what she loved, sent a pang through Haley's heart. For a second the Zina Charles clinic filled her mind, along with all her hopes and dreams for the future.

But that didn't matter. All that mattered was saving Bandit.

Uncle Mike came back in. "Your aunt thinks you're old enough to make this decision," he said. "After all, you worked hard for that money, and you should be able to spend it as you wish. So if you really want to do this, we'll sign off on the surgery."

"Thanks," Haley whispered, relief flooding through her even as she felt her big-time eventing dreams slipping away.

Haley was in a daze for the rest of the morning. Once the paperwork was signed and Dr. Hagen's vet tech had arrived to help prep Bandit for surgery, Uncle Mike had insisted on driving Haley to school.

She didn't have a chance to talk to Tracey and Emma until lunch. When she saw them glaring at her from their usual table, she almost turned and walked the other way. Instead she steeled herself—and marched right over and told them what had happened.

Emma gasped. "Oh no!" she exclaimed, her hands flying to her mouth in horror. "Not Bandit! He's so sweet!"

"Is he going to be all right?" Tracey asked. "I mean, the surgery will fix him, right?"

"Yeah, the vet thinks so." Haley unwrapped her sandwich, though she wasn't hungry.

Just then her phone rang. When Uncle Mike had come in to explain why Haley was late, the school principal had agreed that she could keep the phone on until she'd heard the results of the surgery. Haley's hands shook as she punched the button to answer.

"Good news," Aunt Veronica said, not wasting any time with pleasantries. "Bandit did fine in surgery, and he's resting comfortably at the clinic. Dr. Hagen wants to keep him overnight just as a precaution, but he says we'll be able to bring him home tomorrow."

"Oh, thank goodness!" Haley clutched the phone tightly. "Thanks, Aunt Veronica."

When she hung up, her friends were smiling. "That sounded like good news," Emma said.

"It was. He's going to be okay." Haley smiled too, though it was shaky. Now that Bandit was out of danger, she couldn't seem to stop herself from thinking about what she'd given up to save him. It had been worth it, of course. She'd do it again in a heartbeat—the decision had been easy. But that didn't mean it was easy to accept that she'd just given up her chance to ride with Zina Charles.

"Hey!" Tracey leaned closer, bumping Haley's shoulder with her own. "So why do you still look so bummed out?"

Emma reached across the table and gave Haley's hand a squeeze. "Leave her alone. She's probably still worried about Bandit, right?"

"A little," Haley said. "But the thing is, my aunt and uncle couldn't afford the surgery. So I—I'm the one paying for it. I had to use all the money I saved for the clinic."

"Oh!" Emma's eyes widened, and she glanced over at Tracey as if wondering how to respond.

"Wow," Tracey said. "I can't believe you did that."

Haley shrugged, picking at her sandwich. "What else could I do? I don't regret it." She sighed. "I just wish I didn't have to miss that clinic."

"Yeah." Tracey took a sip of her chocolate milk. "Well, what's done is done, right? I know! We should do something fun this weekend. You know—to take your mind off everything."

"That's a great idea!" Emma exclaimed. "We've barely seen you lately, Haley. It'll be fun!"

Tracey nodded. "Maybe we should hit the mall. Or I know! I can ask my mom to drive us down to Chicago for the day. Won't that be awesome?"

"I guess," Haley murmured. Her friends were being supportive, right? So why did she feel as if they had no idea what she was going through?

That day after school Haley went out to the barn. The beagle mix wandered over to sniff at her shoe, and a couple of cats woke up from their naps and watched her. But the place felt empty without Bandit. And it was all her fault.

She thought about bringing Wings in and going for

a ride, even though it was supposed to be his day off. But what was the point? They didn't need to do trot sets now, or work on their dressage, or even practice their jumping. Not anymore.

The house was just as quiet as the barn. Aunt Veronica had gone grocery shopping, Uncle Mike was at the pharmacy, and both boys had after-school activities that day. Haley glanced at the phone on the kitchen counter, tempted to call Tracey or Emma just to have someone to talk to. But what was the point? Haley's friends obviously didn't understand why she was so upset about giving up the clinic.

Then Haley remembered that there was someone who definitely *would* understand. Three someones, actually.

A moment later she was logging on to the Pony Post. Brooke had posted a picture of her pony eating breakfast, and Nina had written a note about her plans to ride after school. But nobody had checked in yet that afternoon.

Haley was kind of glad that none of the others was on the site just then. She wanted to tell all three of them her news at once.

[HALEY] Hi, guys. Well, I knew there

was a reason I don't like Mondays.

Here's what happened today. . . .

She went on from there, typing out everything that had happened. Bandit. The car. The surgery. And of course, watching her big-time eventing dreams vanish before her eyes.

When she was finished, she sat back and read over what she'd just posted. For the first time all day, the sour feeling in the pit of her stomach faded away. She didn't even need to wait and see what her friends would say. She knew they would understand, and that was all that mattered.

Heading out the back door, she hurried down the path to the main pasture. Wings was grazing with the others, but at Haley's whistle he lifted his head from the grass, stared at her for a moment, and then trotted over. Haley fed the pony a treat, smiling for the first time in hours.

"Hey, buddy," she said, rubbing the pony's fuzzy jaw. Even though the temperatures were still mild, all the horses were already growing their winter coats. "I know it's supposed to be your day off, but I had to see you. How about a ride? No trot sets today—I promise."

Her smile wavered, and tears blurred her vision. Wings was so amazing, and Haley had blown his chance to get even better. But she swallowed back her sadness. It had happened, and she had to accept it. What was the point in worrying about what might have been?

She led Wings to the barn, but tacking up seemed like far too much effort. Instead she just grabbed her helmet and an old schooling bridle and slipped on bareback. This was the good part about not having anything to prepare for. She could just ride her pony and enjoy him, without worrying about accomplishing anything.

That would have to be enough, at least for today.

◆ CHAPTER ◆
11

"OUCH." TRACEY PEERED OVER HALEY'S shoulder as Mr. Washington dropped her math test on her desk. "I can't believe I actually beat you at math for once."

"Don't get used to it," Haley joked weakly, staring at the big, red C-minus at the top of the test paper. True, she wasn't thrilled with the grade. Math might not be her best subject, but she usually managed at least a B average.

But all things considered, she knew she was lucky she'd done that well. She made a mental note to thank Maddie again the next time she logged on to the Pony Post. She hadn't had a chance to check in on the site that morning, since her aunt had sneaked in and turned off her alarm while Haley was still asleep. She'd awakened her just in time to have breakfast and get dressed, telling Haley that the boys had volunteered to take care of all the morning barn chores.

"I thought you could use a little extra sleep today," Aunt Veronica had said, smoothing back the strands of strawberry-blond hair that had plastered themselves to Haley's forehead while she slept.

Haley was touched by her family's kindness. Even though they hadn't said much about either Bandit or the clinic, she could tell they all felt terrible for her. Her friends were being nice about Bandit too, asking about him first thing. But neither of them had even mentioned the clinic. Haley couldn't help wondering if they'd already forgotten all about it.

After school, Haley went with her uncle to pick up Bandit. The dog looked tired, but he sat up and barked when they walked in.

"Easy, Bandit." Uncle Mike smiled and stroked the dog's head. "None of that. You need to rest."

"That's right, Bandit." Haley dropped to her knees and

gave Bandit a hug, being careful not to jostle the cast and splint on his hind leg. "I'm so glad you're going to be okay," she whispered into his fuzzy ear.

The vet tech, a strapping young man who lived just down the road from the Duncans' farm, helped them carry Bandit out to the car. Dr. Hagen walked along, fussing at the tech to be careful.

"You'll need to keep him quiet for a while," the vet told Haley and Uncle Mike. "Give the incision and the bone time to heal."

"Won't be easy," Uncle Mike said with a chuckle. "This one likes to keep moving—sort of like my wife."

That made the vet chuckle too. "Give Veronica my best, will you?" he said. "Anyway, I know you'll do what you can."

As soon as the car pulled up in front of the farmhouse, Jake and Danny dashed out. "Mom borrowed a crate from the Abbots," Danny called. "We just finished setting it up."

"We put it in the kitchen," Jake added. "We figured Bandit would want to be in there, where there's usually people in and out all the time."

For a second Haley wanted to tell them to move the crate up to her room. But she kept quiet, deciding they were right. Bandit would want to be in the center of the action, and that was the kitchen.

The boys and Uncle Mike carried Bandit carefully into the house and set him down in front of the large wire dog crate. "Can he walk?" Danny asked, staring at the cast and splint.

"Doc said he'll be able to hobble around a bit," Uncle Mike said.

"We're not supposed to let him move around much at first, though," Haley added. "Just enough to go out and do his business and stretch his muscles. We should get him into the crate now so he can lie down."

Bandit was staring around the kitchen with interest. He'd been in the house before, of course—all the dogs and most of the cats came in during blizzards and other bad weather. But it had been a while, and he seemed suspicious of the crate, stretching his neck to sniff at the open door while standing back from it as far as possible.

"Go on in, Bandit. It's nice and cozy for you, see?"

Haley patted the folded blanket the boys had put in the crate for him to lie on. Beside the blanket were a water dish and a plate of kibble.

Haley gave the dog a gentle shove to get him started, and Bandit limped into the crate, sniffing at the food. Jake swung the door shut and latched it.

Bandit whined, turning around and pressing his long muzzle against the door.

"Sorry, buddy," Haley said. "I know it'll drive you crazy to be stuck in there. But it's for your own good." She stuck her fingers through the wire, stroking his soft fur.

"How long does he have to stay in there?" Danny asked.

Uncle Mike shrugged. "Doc said it'll take several weeks for Bandit's leg and hip to heal well enough for him to go outside again."

"But the important thing is, he *will* heal," Haley added, smiling as the dog licked her fingers. "Bandit will be as good as new eventually."

Aunt Veronica patted Haley's head. "By the way, in case

we forgot to say it before, we're proud of you for the decision you made, Haley," she said. "It can't have been easy."

"Oh, it was easy." Haley stood up, watching as Bandit sniffed his water. "I mean, what else could I do? It's just too bad . . ."

She let her voice trail off. Why dwell?

Her uncle cleared his throat. "We're sorry we can't help you out with the clinic fee, Haley," he said. "Normally we'd make sure you could still go, let you pay us back or whatnot. It's just not a good time right now."

"I know," Haley said quickly. "And it's okay. But thanks."

She turned away, not wanting them to see her face. As hard as she was trying to move on, forget about that clinic, she was still upset about it. But she didn't want them to think she was upset with them for not being able to loan her the money. Because she wasn't, not at all. The only one she was upset with was herself. She'd made a stupid mistake, and Bandit had almost paid with his life. She couldn't blame anyone else for this.

But I'll get over it, she told herself, kneeling down to

give Bandit another scratch through the wire. *Another clinic will come along. Someday. Maybe.*

Haley knew she needed to call and cancel for the clinic. Somehow, though, as Tuesday turned into Wednesday, she found it impossible to pick up the phone and actually do it. She couldn't quite face that final step just yet.

By the time she got home from school on Wednesday afternoon, though, she knew she couldn't put it off any longer. That wouldn't be fair to the organizers. There was a wait list for riding spots, and they'd be able to find someone to take her place easily enough as long as they had adequate notice. She had to call and tell them she wasn't coming—today.

Haley went upstairs and closed her bedroom door behind her. Pulling out her phone, she sat on the edge of her bed and stared at it. Why couldn't things have worked out differently? She'd worked so hard, gone through so much to earn her spot in the clinic. And all it had taken was one careless moment to see her dreams dashed.

She glanced at her laptop, lying on the desk nearby.

She hadn't so much as peeked at the Pony Post since posting her news on Monday. Even seeing her friends' words of sympathy and support just seemed too hard right now. Maybe she should be grateful that Tracey and Emma already seemed to have forgotten about it. At least that meant she didn't have to talk about it much.

Leaning forward, she touched the laptop cover, tempted to log on now. Maybe her friends could help her figure out how to tell the organizers she was out.

"Don't be silly," she said to herself out loud, sitting back. "I can do this. I *have* to do this."

Not giving herself a chance to waver again, she yanked the clinic flyer off her bulletin board. There was a phone number listed there along with the other contact info, and Haley punched in the numbers as fast as she could, then pressed the phone to her ear, taking a deep breath. It rang three times, and then someone picked up.

"Hello?" a woman's voice said, sounding slightly breathless.

"Hi," Haley said. "Um, I'm calling about the Zina Charles clinic?"

"This is Zina. How can I help you?"

Haley gulped. She hadn't been expecting Zina Charles to answer the phone herself!

"I—oh! I mean, um . . ." She paused, taking another deep breath. She couldn't believe she was actually talking to Zina Charles! "Sorry, um, I didn't think you'd be the one to answer."

Zina's chuckle tickled Haley's ear. "Yes, it's me. And you are?"

"Oh!" Haley felt her cheeks go red and was glad that Zina couldn't see her. "Um, I'm Haley. Haley Duncan?"

"Haley!" Zina sounded delighted. "I'm glad you called. I meant to call you an hour ago, but my big doofus of a gelding managed to pull a shoe, and I've been trying to reach the farrier and just forgot about everything else. Horses! You know how it is." She laughed.

Haley blinked, feeling confused. "Uh—what?"

"Sorry, I'm rambling, aren't I? I do that." Zina chuckled again. "Anyway, what I'm trying to say is, your friends got in touch yesterday and told me what happened. Is your dog okay?"

"My dog?" Haley echoed, more confused than ever now. What friends was Zina talking about? Had Tracey called Zina for some reason? She knew it couldn't have been Emma, who had a near phobia about talking to unfamiliar people on the phone. . . . "Um, he's going to be fine. Thanks."

"I'm a dog lover too, you know," Zina said cheerfully. "Always have a pack running around the barn underfoot! I'd be heartbroken if anything happened to any of the little twerps. So of course when your friends told me about the accident—"

"My friends?" Haley said, her mind spinning as she tried to keep up with Zina's torrent of words. "Which friends?"

"Oh! Well, it was a girl named Nina who e-mailed me. Then I spoke to a Maddie on the phone . . ."

Now things were starting to make more sense. Haley glanced at her laptop again, suddenly wishing she'd logged on to the Pony Post after all. She had the distinct feeling she might have missed something important.

"Am I talking too fast and mixing things up?" Zina

asked. "I do that. Sorry! Anyway, your friend Maddie explained about the surgery and the money and how hard you've been working and all that. She talks almost as fast as I do, actually—could hardly get a word in edgewise!" She laughed again. "She and your other friends were already coming up with plans to send me the money in installments and all sorts of other stuff. Took me three or four tries to get through to her and tell her I had a better idea."

"You—you did?" Haley pressed the phone to her ear, still totally confused, but also touched and amazed that her Pony Post friends had gone to so much effort to try to help.

"Yes," Zina went on. "See, nobody gets anywhere in this sport on their own, right? I had some super-generous people who helped me out along the way, especially in the early days when I was struggling to get my first horse past training level. I've never forgotten about that, and I believe in paying it forward."

"Paying it forward?" Haley echoed, feeling a glimmer of hope well up inside her.

"That's why I'm making you an offer," Zina said. "If you're willing to get there early and stay late and work really hard in between, you can keep your spot in the clinic. No charge."

Haley couldn't believe her ears. "Can you repeat that, please?"

"I said, you're in," Zina said. "You can still ride in the clinic. If you're interested, that is."

"Are you serious? Of course I'm interested! I'll do it!" Haley exclaimed.

"Make sure you know what you're accepting, Haley." Zina's tone was serious, though there was a hint of a smile in it. "I'm not kidding about the hard work. There's going to be a ton to do, and I need someone who's willing to do it all—jump crew, gopher, groom, manure removal specialist, whatever."

"I'll do it!" Haley echoed, a smile spreading across her face. "I'll do anything, I swear!"

"Good." Zina sounded pleased. "I'll text you the details later. By the way, I can't wait to meet your pony. I rode a Chincoteague once in a lesson barn, and of course

I read *Misty of Chincoteague* and all those other books over and over again as a kid."

"Me too." Haley glanced across the room at her bookshelf, where her favorite horse novels held a place of honor on the top shelf.

"Listen, I've got to go, I think that's the farrier on the other line. But I'll see you Saturday, right?" Zina said. "I'll e-mail you later to confirm times and stuff."

"Yes! Okay. See you then. Oh! And thanks so much! This is going to be amazing!"

"You're welcome. Bye, Haley."

"Bye." Haley hung up, still hardly believing this was happening—that her dream was going to come true after all. And she had her Pony Post friends to thank for it! With a smile, she wondered who had come up with the idea of contacting Zina directly. Probably Nina—she wasn't afraid of talking to anyone, plus she met famous and successful people all the time, thanks to her parents' cool careers. Then again, maybe it had been Maddie, who wasn't exactly shy herself and was the type of person to jump right in and try to fix things. Or maybe Brooke? She was a lot quieter than the other two, but she was smart and good at seeing possibilities that other people might miss.

It probably doesn't even matter, Haley told herself. *The important thing is, they came through for me. All three of them. And I'm never ever going to forget it!* She knew she should sign on and start thanking them immediately. But she was so excited and happy and filled with energy that she wasn't sure she could sit still right then. Besides, there was someone else who needed to hear the news. . . .

Five minutes later she was ducking between the fence boards of the pasture. She raced over to Wings, who was dozing with the other horses in the shade of the pines along the fence line.

"Wings, guess what?" Haley cried, flinging her arms around his neck. "It's back on, buddy! We're going to that clinic!"

• CHAPTER •
12

"IS THIS IT?" UNCLE MIKE LEANED FORWARD over the steering wheel, peering at a sign looming out of the early-morning fog.

"That's it!" Haley bounced on the truck's passenger seat, wide awake despite the early hour. She glanced back at the trailer bumping along behind them. "Thanks again for skipping your fishing meeting to drive me to the clinic, Uncle Mike."

He glanced over. "Welcome. Wouldn't trust anyone else to get that pony of yours here in one piece."

Haley smiled at him, knowing there was more to it than that. Her entire family was being so great she could hardly stand it. The boys had woken up early to help her load her tack trunk into the truck and Wings into the trailer, promising to take care of all her chores while she was away.

"You don't even have to pay us," Danny had added with a yawn.

The host farm was a fancy place with two large barns, a separate dressage court, an indoor ring, and a huge all-weather jumping ring. Behind all that, Haley knew, an extensive cross-country course wound its way through the hills and fields. The farm hosted several recognized events per season, and Haley hoped that one day she and Wings would be good enough to compete there.

"Looks like this is the place," Uncle Mike commented, pulling up beside several other rigs. Most of them included large, fancy goosenecks or gleaming aluminum trailers with dressing rooms. But there were a couple of other more humble setups like their own, too. Beside one of them, a willowy teenage girl was brushing a pretty gray mare. When Haley hopped out of the cab of the truck, the teen glanced over, smiled, and waved before returning to her grooming.

Haley waved back, then hurried around to check on Wings. Moments later she was leading him into one of the barns, following the directions of a harried-seeming young man with a clipboard.

Soon she'd settled the pony in his temporary stall with a hay net she'd brought from home. When she emerged, the young man was rushing past, carrying a bucket.

"Um, is Zina around?" Haley called to him. "I should probably check in with her."

"You can sign in out by the ring." The man sounded distracted, verging on annoyed. "The secretary will take your check and get you your info packet."

"Wait—but Zina told me I should find her as soon as I got here." Haley was a little intimidated by the man's brisk manner, but she wasn't going to let that stop her. "Um, I'm Haley?"

"Haley?" Suddenly the young man's entire demeanor changed. He smiled at Haley, still looking harried but now also relieved. "Why didn't you say so? Thank goodness you're here! Here—take this to Zina." He shoved the bucket at her. "She's up at the house."

Haley hurried toward the large, imposing brick house behind the barn, following the sound of voices to a propped-open door leading into a spacious country kitchen. Inside, Zina was leaning against the counter sipping coffee and talking to several other adults. She looked just like she did in all the pictures and videos Haley had seen of her. She was around thirty, with dark-brown hair pulled back from her round, cheerful face in a short ponytail. Her boots and breeches were clean, but there was a smudge of dirt beneath one eye and several pieces of hay in her hair.

"Haley!" Zina exclaimed when Haley introduced herself. "I'm so glad you're here! Guys, this is the girl I told you about."

The other adults surveyed Haley with interest. Most of them looked like riders too. They ranged in age from slightly younger than Zina to almost as old as Haley's grandparents. Zina introduced them, talking so fast that Haley only caught about half the names and forgot even those almost immediately. She settled for smiling and saying hello, and that seemed to be fine.

"Okay, let's get started." Zina set down her coffee cup and clapped her hands, her eyes sparkling with excitement. "Ready to work, Haley?"

"Ready!" Haley said with a smile.

The next hour or two passed in a crazy, confusing, strenuous, wonderful rush. Haley stayed busy helping horses and riders settle in, finding lost bits of tack, hauling hay and water around, picking out stalls, running paperwork back and forth to the house, and fetching coffee.

The clinic was divided into three different sets of riders grouped by experience. Each group would spend almost three hours with Zina, learning more about dressage, show jumping, and cross-country in turn. The first group was the most experienced, and the horses and riders took Haley's breath away as they warmed up for their dressage lesson.

"Haley!" The harried young man, whose name Haley had learned was Archie, rushed up to her. "More coffee."

"Got it." Haley sprinted toward the house, returning moments later with a travel mug of steaming-hot coffee.

Zina was already in the ring, watching the riders warm up. "You're a lifesaver!" she exclaimed, reaching for the mug. "It'd be awfully embarrassing if I fell asleep during the first session."

Several of the riders were close enough to hear her and chuckle. Haley laughed too. "What do you need me to do now?" she asked Zina.

"Catch your breath and watch for a bit, why don't you," Zina suggested. "Keep an eye on the woman on the big chestnut over there—she's ridden with me before, and they really know their stuff. Used to compete in straight dressage before they got bored with that and joined the dark side."

Haley nodded. "Are you sure? I'm supposed to be working to earn my spot, so . . ."

"Don't worry." Zina chuckled. "You'll be back to work soon enough. But I always learned almost as much by watching as by riding myself, eh?"

Haley nodded and smiled her thanks. Zina took a sip of her coffee, then strode to the center of the ring and called for attention.

"All right, everyone, welcome!" she said loudly. "If everyone's warmed up, let's get this party started. . . ."

"Excellent!" Zina exclaimed as a stout woman on an even stouter Morgan cross mare sailed over a vertical jump made up of red-and-white-striped rails. The intermediate group was halfway through its show jumping session. "Now let's put the final element up a couple of holes and try it again, everyone. Haley?"

"Got it!" Haley sprang into action, rushing over from her spot on the rail. She quickly adjusted the fence, pulling out the jump pins that held the cups in place on the standards and replacing them two holes higher. Then she stepped back as Zina signaled for the first rider in line to begin.

Haley had no idea what time it was, though Archie had shoved a sandwich and a soda into her hand sometime between the intermediates' dressage and show jumping sessions. She had gulped down the food as fast as she could and gone right back to work, setting up the gymnastic exercise Zina had described to her. Her mind was buzzing with everything she'd learned so far just by watching the other riders between tasks. Seeing the advanced group on cross-country had been amazing! Zina had driven herself and Haley out there in a golf cart, and Haley had been in charge of stomping down any divots the horses' hooves left in the carefully manicured turf.

She hoped Zina would let her come along to watch the intermediates on cross-country too. But as the show jumping session ended, the clinician called Haley over. "Time to hit the barn, girl," she said.

"Oh." Haley tried not to let her disappointment show. After all, she was supposed to be working, not watching. "Okay. What do you want me to do?"

Zina smiled. "Um, how about tacking up that cute pony of yours?" she said. "He's been standing in that stall all day, so you'll want plenty of time for a good warm-up before your dressage session starts."

"Oh!" Haley had almost forgotten that she and Wings were riding in the third and final group. Her heart thumped with excitement. "Sure. I mean okay. I mean, let me know if you need me to do anything else or whatever."

"Go." Zina grinned. "I'll see you in the dressage ring in an hour."

"Go, go, go!" Zina shouted, clapping her hands. "Don't let him slow down—he's been through the water like three times now, he doesn't have an excuse!"

Haley gave Wings a brisk kick. "Get up!" she growled. They were working on hopping over one of the log jumps built into the edge of the farm's water jump, a broad, shallow pool with a sandy bottom. The horses were meant to canter up to the jump, taking off on dry ground and landing in the water. That was one type of jump that Haley hadn't been able to figure out how to build at home, so Wings wasn't quite sure what to make of it. Luckily, he wasn't the only one. Of the four other pairs in the group, only one of the horses had much experience jumping into water.

"We go swimming in the cow pond back home," a cheerful woman in her late twenties had volunteered with a smile. "Does that count?"

Haley had laughed. "We do that too!"

She was still a little amazed by how friendly everyone was. Haley was the youngest rider of the bunch, and Wings the shortest equine. But the others, from a bashful teenage boy with rosy cheeks and a lanky bay Thoroughbred to a woman in her sixties who was an experienced foxhunter and enthusiastic new event rider, all accepted Haley as one of them—an eventer and a horse person.

The horses' hesitance at the water jump didn't seem to bother Zina at all. She'd had Haley and the other riders walk into and through the pool a few times first with no jump involved, letting their horses get their feet wet and sniff at the water. One horse had even lowered his head to take a long drink!

Then there was the sweet-eyed chestnut gelding ridden by a nervous middle-aged woman. When she let him stop in the middle of the pool, he stuck his nose into the water and pawed at it a few times.

"Um, you might want to kick him forward," Zina suggested.

Haley nodded. She could tell what the horse was

thinking—that the nice, cool water seemed like a fine place to roll!

"Go on, Star." The rider gave a tentative kick, which the horse completely ignored. With a grunt, he buckled his knees and started to drop.

"Star, no!" Haley was close enough to reach out and give the horse a tap on the rump with her crop. That startled him enough to make him pause—and Zina enough time to wade in and grab him by the bridle, dragging him forward out of the water.

"Oh my!" the rider exclaimed, looking sheepish. "Sorry about your boots, Zina! But thanks—I wasn't in the mood for a swim."

That made everyone laugh, including Zina. "It's all right, these boots have been through worse," she assured the woman. Then she glanced at Haley. "Quick thinking, Haley. Thanks."

"Yes, thank you!" Star's rider added with a smile.

Haley smiled back. Even though everyone took learning and improving seriously, it was nice to see that they all had a sense of humor, too!

But Haley wasn't thinking about any of that as she and Wings approached the jump into the water. Several strides out the pony's trot slowed slightly, his ears pricking forward. Would he do it? For a moment Haley imagined Wings skidding to a stop and tossing her headfirst into the water.

She shook off those thoughts quickly. Wings had never let her down before—and she knew he wouldn't start now. "Go on, boy!" she yelled, booting him forward again. "You can do it!"

And he did! His stride picked up, and he took off over the log with several inches to spare.

He landed with a splash, tossing his head and snorting as he cantered off through the shallow water.

"Good boy!" Zina shouted. "Well ridden, Haley. Did you see that, everyone? That's how you do it!"

Haley grinned, giving Wings a pat as she pulled him back to a walk at the far end of the pool. "That was awesome!" she exclaimed. "Good boy, Wingsie!"

"Wake up, Haley. We're home."

Haley opened her eyes, which she'd sworn she was just

going to rest for a second. Blinking sleepily, she realized her uncle was right. They were home.

She yawned and smiled, thinking back over the long, busy, tiring, exciting day. The clinic had been everything she'd hoped it would be. Maybe more, actually. Working alongside Zina all day had given Haley a taste of what an upper-level event rider's life was really like. It was hard to believe how much hard work, how many details, went into the whole business of running a clinic! She could only imagine that a competition would be even more hectic and intense.

She could only imagine it for now, anyway. Someday soon, she hoped she and Wings could use what they'd just learned by competing in another event, maybe a recognized one this time.

Zina certainly seemed to think they could do it. At the end of the day, Haley had helped her pack up her equipment. While they were working, they'd had a chance for a real talk. Zina had been encouraging of Haley's dreams for herself and for Wings.

"Do you really think we can make it?" Haley had

asked, shooting Zina a sidelong glance as she lowered the rider's grooming bucket into the trunk of her rental car.

"All the elements are there for you." Zina had slammed the trunk shut and turned to face Haley, squinting in the lowering dusk. "You've got a good, brave, athletic pony who'd do anything for you. You've got determination and a great work ethic. Just make sure you don't work so hard that you burn yourself out."

"What do you mean?" Haley had asked. "Doing all this . . ." She'd waved a hand at the farm around them. "It's not like work at all. It's fun!"

"I know. But your friends told me a little about everything you were doing to earn money to come." Zina's expression was serious now as she peered at Haley. "You have to be careful not to push yourself too hard."

"Run myself ragged," Haley murmured. "That's what my aunt says."

Zina smiled. "Your aunt sounds like a smart lady. And don't get me wrong, Haley. If you want to make it in this sport, you've got to be tough and work hard. Just make sure you keep some balance in your life too, you know?

Other hobbies, fun with friends, some time off—you told me you give your pony a day off every week, right? Make sure you take the same kind of care of yourself, that's all I'm saying."

For a second, Haley wanted to protest. Zina had worked and pushed and struggled to reach the top—she said so in every interview Haley had ever read about her. She'd just admitted it now, at least sort of.

But maybe it wasn't as simple as that. Haley had trusted Zina to help her get Wings through that water jump. Shouldn't she trust her on this, too?

Zina was watching her. "Do you understand what I'm saying, Haley? I'm not telling you to stop trying your best or anything like that. You're like me—that part comes naturally. I'm just saying there's more to life than all this." She waved a hand to indicate the darkened stables. "I don't want you to forget that. Promise me you'll think about it?"

"Sure." Haley had smiled uncertainly at her idol, still not quite sure what to think.

Now, as she led Wings into his stall, Haley found

herself thinking about Zina's words again. She'd learned a lot from Zina over the course of the day, but she was starting to have a funny feeling that the stuff about balance might have been one of the most important lessons of all.

"Maybe she's right, Wingsie," she said as she glanced into the pony's water bucket, glad to see that someone had topped it off earlier. "The clinic was great, and I can't wait to start practicing some of the stuff we learned. But first, I'm thinking maybe we could both use a few days off. What do you think? We'll take it easy, go for a relaxing trail ride or two. I think there's a team penning next weekend—we could go and show Owen Lemke how it's done, huh?"

That made her think about Tracey and Emma. Maybe she could use a few days off to reconnect with them, too. She grimaced as she thought about what Zina had said. Maybe Haley's friends weren't the only ones who hadn't been trying hard enough. Come to think of it, Haley hadn't exactly tried too hard to get involved with any of the stuff Tracey and Emma cared about these days either.

She hadn't even asked them about the school dance they'd been so excited about.

"Oops," she whispered, stroking Wings's neck. "Maybe I haven't been that good of a friend lately."

She felt a twinge of guilt. So what if she wasn't as boy crazy as her friends? They weren't horse crazy at all, and they still made an effort to ask her about Wings now and then. The least she could do was try to meet them halfway. Maybe that was the kind of thing Zina was talking about—balance. Paying attention to *everything* that was important to her.

Wings snuffled at her pocket, looking for treats. Haley rubbed his ears and then pushed him gently away, letting herself out of the stall.

"Good night, Wings," she called. "See you in the morning."

She hurried out of the barn and across the yard, rubbing her arms. It was turning chilly, the cool night breeze cutting the lingering warmth of the day with a hint of coming winter. The kitchen felt warm and cozy when Haley let herself in.

"Hey, Bandit," she said softly. "Easy—no barking! Everyone else is asleep."

The dog whined, pushing himself into an upright position on his good leg. His tail slapped the bars of the crate as Haley swung open the door to give him a pat.

"Good boy," she whispered. "You're such a good boy!"

She spent a few minutes with him, but finally she couldn't stop yawning, so she closed him in his crate with a couple of treats and headed upstairs. Her bed looked comfortable and inviting. But there was one thing she needed to do before she went to sleep.

Soon she was logging on to the Pony Post. She'd checked in the other day after talking to Zina, of course, and ever since, most of the posts had been about the clinic. There were several new messages waiting for her, all posted that afternoon and evening.

[MADDIE] I wonder what H. is doing RIGHT NOW?

[BROOKE] Easy—she & Wings
are having a blast! lol!

[NINA] So true! I can't wait to

hear all about the clinic.

[MADDIE] Me too—hint hint, Haley!

[NINA] lol, relax. She said she'd prob.

be home late, remember?

[BROOKE] Ya, I think the place the

clinic was being held was like half

an hour away or something.

[MADDIE] whatevs. I just hope she fills us in soon!

[BROOKE] lol, maybe she should've worn a

helmet cam so u could watch the whole thing!

[MADDIE] Ooh! What an awesome idea!

Why didn't I think of that sooner???

[BROOKE] lol!

[NINA] LOL from me too! Anyway,

Haley, whenever us see this, I hope u

had the time of your life today!

"I did," Haley whispered, opening a new text box. She sat there with her fingers poised over the keyboard for a moment, trying to figure out how to describe the day. Finally she started to type.

[HALEY] I'm about to fall asleep on my feet.

But I wanted to check in w/you guys and say

that today was INCREDIBLE!!!!!! Zina is the best.

Riding w/her made me even more excited to

keep going & working my way up the levels

w/Wings. I'll tell u all the details tomorrow—

maybe we can even get our parents to let

us have a group phone call? B/c I'm dying to

tell u guys everything—esp. since you're the

whole reason it happened! THANK U THANK

U THANK U—u are the best friends ever!!!!!!!!!!

She sent the message with a smile, knowing that her friends would all see it first thing tomorrow. About ten seconds later she was falling into bed, not bothering to set the alarm for once. Five seconds after that she was drifting off to sleep, already dreaming.

◆ Glossary ◆

Chincoteague pony: A breed of pony found on Assateague Island, which lies off the coasts of Maryland and Virginia. Chincoteague ponies are sometimes referred to as wild horses, but are more properly called "feral" since they are not native to the island but were brought there by humans sometime many years past. There are several theories about how this might have happened, including the one told in the classic novel *Misty of Chincoteague* by Marguerite Henry. That novel also details the world-famous pony swim and auction that still take place in the town of Chincoteague to this day.

barrel racing: A rodeo event. A horse and rider must perform a specific pattern around three barrels, and the team with the fastest time wins.

cinch: The strap that holds a Western saddle on a horse. The cinch can be made of cord, nylon, or various other materials.

clinic: An intensive lesson, usually involving several riders and a well-known trainer.

cross-country: One of the three phases of eventing, in which a horse is asked to jump a timed course of solid obstacles. The object is to complete the course with as few time and jumping penalties as possible. Unlike the other two phases, cross-country is unique to eventing.

eventing: A sport in which horse and rider must complete three separate phases: dressage, cross-country, and show jumping.

ground tying: Despite the name, this doesn't involve tying at all. It's when a horse is trained to remain in one place without being tied or otherwise secured.

hay net: A hay net is exactly what it sounds like—a net that holds hay! It can be hung in a stall, in a trailer, or on a fence to prevent a horse from stepping on or otherwise soiling or wasting the hay.

leg yield: A basic dressage move in which a horse moves forward and sideways at the same time.

muzzle: This word has two meanings involving horses. The muzzle is a part of the horse's head incorporating the mouth and nose. A muzzle is also a device that fits over the horse's muzzle to prevent it from eating too fast, or from biting.

roll top: A type of cross-country jump with a rounded top.

team penning: A Western sport based on ranch work, in which teams of riders must separate cattle from a herd and maneuver them into a pen.

Trakehner: A type of cross-country jump consisting of a rail positioned over a ditch.

Marguerite Henry's Ponies of Chincoteague is inspired by the award-winning books by Marguerite Henry, the beloved author of such classic horse stories as *King of the Wind*; *Misty of Chincoteague*; *Justin Morgan Had a Horse*; *Stormy, Misty's Foal*; *Misty's Twilight*; and *Album of Horses*, among many other titles.

Learn more about the world of Marguerite Henry at www.MistyofChincoteague.org.

Don't miss the next book in the series!

Book 4: *Moonlight Mile*